LOVE AND DEATH

A sort of spasm passed over Mrs. Grahn's face.

She cried out, "He didn't die of his heart, he was killed, murdered in his bed," the words tumbling over each other now, the voice even higher, "and it had to be one of you, here, he hadn't an enemy in the world, everybody loved him—"

Jack's quiet voice asked, "But why, Mrs. Grahn? Why do you say that?"

"Because he was going to marry me."

Triumphant, shoulders squared. She was breathing hard.

"The woman's been drinking," Marcia said to Leo.

"—Yes, marry me. That's right, stare. Mr. Philip Andrew Converse marrying his housekeeper? But someone heard about it, someone killed him, someone right here murdered him in his bed—"

Books by Mary McMullen
from Jove

THE GIFT HORSE
SOMETHING OF THE NIGHT
A GRAVE WITHOUT FLOWERS
UNTIL DEATH DO US PART
THE OTHER SHOE
BETTER OFF DEAD
THE BAD-NEWS MAN
THE DOOM CAMPAIGN
A COUNTRY KIND OF DEATH
THE PIMLICO PLOT
STRANGLE HOLD
FUNNY, JONAS, YOU DON'T LOOK DEAD
A DANGEROUS FUNERAL

Watch for

PRUDENCE BE DAMNED

coming in January!

A DANGEROUS FUNERAL

MARY McMULLEN

JOVE BOOKS, NEW YORK

This Jove book contains the complete
text of the original hardcover edition.
It has been completely reset in a typeface
designed for easy reading, and was printed
from new film.

A DANGEROUS FUNERAL

A Jove Book / published by arrangement with Doubleday,
a division of Bantam Doubleday Dell Publishing Group, Inc.

PRINTING HISTORY
Jove edition / December 1988

ISBN: 0-515-09845-0

Jové Books are published by The Berkley Publishing Group,
200 Madison Avenue, New York, New York 10016.
The name "JOVE" and the "J" logo
are trademarks belonging to Jove Publications, Inc.

PRINTED IN THE UNITED STATES OF AMERICA

10 9 8 7 6 5 4 3 2 1

To Alton

ONE

"Oh Lord, oh, *frightful*, dear Phip," Marcia said, the syllables falling away, leaves from her tree. And then she rallied and added in her practical way, "But what an inconvenient place to die."

Philip Andrew Converse's death in North Truro, Massachusetts, occured late on Tuesday night or early Wednesday morning. No one was exactly sure of the time.

Telephone calls were made, directions given and followed.

He had always been a considerate man. "If I know that lot, they'll be all over the place. Give them time to get to me. And don't streamline anything, I want a nice old-fashioned binge."

It had taken, two Christmases back, a good deal of whiskey to get up his courage to give his younger brother and lawyer, Leo Converse, instructions concerning the ceremonies that would follow his demise.

". . . Of course, it may be years, let's say even decades, but it's just as well to get rid of the matter while I'm still sound. The plainest, cheapest coffin they've got—ah well, that just about finishes it. Let's have a refill."

Over the refill, "Except—flowers, yes, don't trouble yourself with 'please omit,' it's one of the honored pastimes. People liking to see how their own arrived, did they get their money's worth, and disparaging somebody else's carnations or roses— 'Did they pick them up at a stand in the subway, I wonder?'—

1

and in general having a fine time going around the room and pricing baskets and wreaths.

"Yes, when they've finished resting your soul, and telling stories about you, good and bad, there are always the flowers, before they come back to the living and have at each other. For a reviving bit of sport."

He looked at his glass. "Good God, this must have a leak in it, it's empty again. I've been meaning to tell you for years, Leo, that you look like an Irishman painted by El Greco. A very merry Christmas to you."

The wake would occupy Thursday and Friday. The burial would take place Saturday morning.

"Don't stick them with a solemn requiem mass. Low will do nicely. Many's the high one I've suffered through, thinking if I had to bow my head one more time it would fall off into the next pew. . . ."

"Are you going up?" Kate Converse asked her cousin Sophie, over the telephone.

"Goin' *up!* I wouldn't miss that beanfeast for worlds. Poor darlin' Phip, of course, *he'll* hate missin' it, but the God-blessed old bastard even with two heart attacks landed standin' upright with both feet on the age of seventy-two before he copped it."

Sophie, president of Sophie Converse, Inc., was a most unlikely light of New York's garment district, Seventh Avenue. Her drawl suggested, particularly when some of the earthiness was omitted, mint juleps on a pillared porch, great shady straw hats with floating ribbons, cucumber lotions to keep a lady's skin pink and fair, and a honeyed heat misting the live oaks.

She was at thirty-nine an extraordinarily successful business-woman and designer of clothes that retailed from $500 to $2,500 at good stores from New York to California, and in Mexico, Canada, and South America.

"You come on along with me, Kate. Drive'd be a drag. I'll have some minion get us on a Boston plane and from there we'll hire a flyin' machine that may or not make it to Province-town."

As with all sudden announcements of even more or less

expected deaths, Kate at first felt nothing; the news about her Uncle Phip hadn't hit bottom but had just made its first splash in her pool.

Phip, a rich man not cut to pattern. She supposed fortunes were not made by the exercise of a general benevolence toward all; but to his family kind, impulsive, open-handed. Both his houses always wide and welcoming: the town house on Eighty-third Street; the place in North Truro, on Cape Cod, which from her earliest years brought to Kate's mental nose a scent of salt and sea grass and roses.

He had gotten a full column on the obituary page of the New York *Times*. Proper attention was paid to his notable career in real estate and land development.

The string of Hearth Homes, coast to coast, Come Home to Us and Light Your Own Hearthfire. (Ruinous, competitors had wailed, the insurance alone—but Phip had his own company in his back pocket, Confire, to insure his motels.) Canalways Villages, watery, romantic, and expensive, in fifteen states. And the thunderous might of Converse Triple Towers soaring above the Narrows.

But the real juice of the story was his discreetly famed collection of French Impressionists and Post-Impressionists. The *Times* could not list the full inventory, as only Philip Converse knew that; but it confidently mentioned Matisse, Picasso, Renoir, Degas, Monet, and Manet.

Disliking herself, Kate thought, My God, there'll be an awful lot of money involved in this. . . .

Phip had once said to her, "They'll go on sale after my death, of course. I only wish I could watch the scramble. It's selfish to keep them bottled up—and I've had the pleasure of them to myself for a long, long time."

". . . survived by a sister, Mrs. Daniel Dalrymple; his brothers, New York Democratic Senator Garrett Converse; Leo Converse, partner in the firm of Leavings, Radnor, Currie and Converse; Hugh Converse, Hong Kong export-import dealer. His family includes a niece, Sophie Converse, the fashion designer; a niece, Angela Converse, a model; a nephew, John Converse, who is with the Washington Bureau of the New York *Times*; a nephew, Vincent Converse, a vice-president of

Jesup and Laird, Inc.; and grand-nephews and nieces.''

They've skipped me completely, Kate thought. But she supposed that as a mere group head at Mall and Mall, Advertising, she didn't rate inclusion by the *Times* in the roster of better-known Converses. And of course she wasn't a real Converse at all; she was an adopted one.

But she felt real enough; she had been only two years old when her father and mother had been killed in a car smash and her father's closest friend, Hugh Converse, had driven over at two in the morning and dropped the baby-sitter at home and carried the small wrapped sleeping bundle to his house, not just for the one disastrous night but for good.

And Phip, too, between her coffee and her shower, was beginning to feel real too, sadly real, dead in his house that smelled of salt and roses.

It did not occur to Leo Converse to telephone his son, Timothy, or his daughter, Angela—renamed by him, in forgotten love when she was three days old, Tike. They would no doubt read about it in the *Times*. That is, if they ever read anything.

In any case, Timothy hadn't a telephone, and whenever he had an occasion to call Tike, she was seldom at home but at work in, according to her answering service, St. Tropez or Antigua or the Isle of Skye.

He called his eldest nephew, Vincent Converse.

"Bad news, Vin. Phip.''

A silence. "Oh, Christ,'' Vin said, his voice hoarse. "The other shoe.''

"You sound bad—a cold, the flu?'' Leo was a mild hypochondriac and disliked the idea of catching something uncomfortable at Phip's coffinside.

"No, an obscure disease called J and B fever, not communicable until the bottle cap is removed. Can I drive you up?''

In Leo's view, Vin at the wheel of a car was like a failed jockey trying to make a comeback.

"Thank you, no,'' he said hastily. "I'll take the Boston plane. There's that helicopter service from Wall Street, to Kennedy. . . .''

Vin laughed a little and then choked the sound back.

"I suppose now — God rest his soul — expense is no object."

To his wife, Glenna, Vin said, "Brace yourself, sober clothes and too much to drink all around, me especially — Phip's been gathered up. Dead. Leo's handling everything."

In the bathroom, five minutes later, Glenna splashed her face with palmfuls of cold water, trying to wash away the swollen redness of her tears of joy.

"Oh thank God thank God thank God. . . ."

"Come one, come all," Sophie chanted, fastening her seat belt on the Boston plane.

She had been a good deal stared at while boarding. She was a splendidly tall woman, broad-shouldered, narrow-waisted. Her nose was forthright, her forehead high, wide, and rounded under a careless billow of soft straw-gold hair that seemed to have its own wind moving in it.

She had the blue Converse eyes, a wide thin-lipped mouth — a curiously ironic mouth, for a woman — and radiantly translucent fair skin. She wore a pants suit of crisp silk thinly striped in brown and white, with a striped long scarf that floated in her wake like a banner. Over one arm was slung a cape of russet suede lined in sable.

Kate, beside her, was far less instantly noticeable.

"Does it ever bother you, Sophie, everybody looking and wondering who in the devil you are?" she asked.

"Not at all. Borrowin' from Mr. Mailer, it's my business to be an advertisement for myself. Hence the first-class seats. Make yourself comfortable, they're on me. An Incorporated does not travel second class."

Adjusting her scarf with a great clanking of bracelets — the hands were nervous, the voice was not — she went on with relish, "I declare I can hardly wait to get my arms around the First Prize and give him a real big old hug." This being her designation for their cousin John Converse.

"Do you suppose he can get away from Washington?"

"Wild horses wouldn't hold him. I feel it safe to predict everybody will come flockin', from the highways and the by-ways and out from under damp stones. I do hope and sincerely pray that trashy Tike can't make it, especially considerin' that every hour away from the camera lens costs her at least a hundred dollars.''

Kate thought about absolutely nothing during takeoff, except, as usual, Will we make it this time? Again? Or will we just roar on like this forever, until we hit something, on the ground—

Funny that when you watched other people's jets take off, they seemed to shoot straight up into the air; but when you were on them, time stopped and the runway seemed at least ten miles long.

At the blessed lifting when the earth dropped from the wheels, she considered with casual disfavor her cousin Tike. At twenty, a model, The Model, current darling of fashion editors and photographers. Kate was twenty-nine but she thought of herself as being, in a way, of a whole other generation than Tike's. They seldom met, and never by choice or arrangement; the last time she had seen Tike had been at a party six months ago, at which Tike had arrived with four variously assorted men, one, she remembered, being a weight lifter and another a tall sandy-haired Australian whom Tike introduced to the room at large as ''the tennis player Joe Cox and I mean *Cox!*''

Sophie signaled the stewardess. ''A little champagne to soothe us in the event of turbulence. Two splits, please, thank you kindly.''

Sipping thirstily, she said, ''Well, what's your scenario? Mine is Marcia examinin' the tops of the picture frames for dust and busily rappin' knuckles. There will be at least one bitch of a battle, fisticuffs highly probable, and several severe lacerations. At least two good folk will decide not to speak to each other for a year. And we can expect frontal, flank, and rear attacks on the bottle table.''

Like most large clans of Irish persuasion, the Converses were no strangers to often vivid wakes and funerals. The last two years had been quiet, however; everybody, if not thriving, surviving.

Kate found herself very much looking forward to seeing the First Prize.

It must have been over a year since they had last met, at the wedding of a mutual second cousin, one of the Dalrymples, but they hadn't had more than a word or two together. He had had one of his spectacular girls with him, and had been thoroughly occupied with her.

Even in a handsome and talented and brainy family, Jack had a special place of his own.

At Sophie's birthday party, several months before the Dalrymple wedding, Sophie had murmured under music to Kate, on Jack's entrance, his arms decorated with a huge bunch of white lilacs and a cream and lavender Siamese kitten as a present for her, "Strike up the band. Ignite the rockets. Here comes a man. A real honest-to-God celebration of the sex politely but often *in*accurately known as male."

Well, southern of her, Kate had thought; delightfully and affectionately family, no wonder and worry about being suspected of the rustle of incestuous sheets. She wished she were not so calmly buttoned up, reserved; that she could fling, as Sophie did, an open joy at a reunion with an agreeable cousin. Any agreeable cousin, of course. Not just the First Prize.

Thinking about Sophie and Jack, and love hidden and withheld through shyness, or good manners, or lack of practice, she was caught back suddenly to her last time with Phip. Of course, she hadn't known it would be the last time.

They were sitting under the catalpa tree on the shallow front lawn, the strange immense tree that went straight up, split into two great symmetrical limbs, and exploded in sunlit green far overhead; it had always reminded her of a mysterious and noble sculpture, a man, upside down, head buried deep in the earth and legs powerfully aloft.

"Why aren't you married, Kate?"

The familiar question. Kind, well meant; but always a little intrusive.

Phip in his striped canvas hammock chair, face pink-tan, merry conniving blue eyes looking at her a little anxiously, fine blade of a nose, thick white hair cut in not at all an elderly way, seersucker trousers, faded blue shirt, glass in his hand tinkling.

"I suppose the contemporary answer is, why on earth should I be?" she had said.

"You're a warm woman, Kate. Girl, I should say. You'd

make a nice wife. And very good-looking of course, but in a way, that's beside the point.''

He paused, and looked at a blue butterfly investigating the rank-smelling white blossoms of the tall privet hedge. ''People should marry. If only to comfort each other.''

''From where I sit, that's rather a thin reason,'' and then an instant feeling of shame at flaunting her young health before her uncle. Although, thin as he was, boneless as he was, he looked remarkably young himself for his years and anything but ill.

''No it isn't, Kate. Lovers are all very well, and yes, I do know what year it is. But who's to worry about you if you have an unattractive cold in your head, or your breakfast toast is burnt, or you've stubbed your toe in the dark and hurt yourself?''

She had for a moment the feeling that he was not addressing her at all, but someone else.

Probably the sleepy heat, and her lunchtime martinis.

''Or,'' Phip went on dreamily, talking to the butterfly, ''forgive you your hangover and hold your head even though *they* don't have one. And remember things like, you relish just the merest pinch of nutmeg in your creamed potatoes. . . .''

''You never married.''

''The only woman I ever wanted to marry had other ideas. That's a long story, I won't bore you with it.''

Telling long rambling stories about anything was considered a mortal sin among the impatient quick-witted Converses; and in the unlikely event that you dared to try to sketch the plot of a book or a movie, you faced being cast into absolute outer darkness.

She remembered looking at her watch. Her friends at Orleans, with whom she had been spending the weekend, would be picking her up at any minute for Sunday cocktails and dinner.

Out of the two whole days, she had found only one hour to offer to Phip.

He followed her glance at her wrist. ''Am I scaring you off, talking about marriage? Well, single or in any other state, you're always welcome here, Kate, and for a good deal longer than this bat of an eyelash—''

Her friends' car stopping at the opening in the center of the privet hedge. A hasty bending over, hugging Phip's thin shoulders, a kiss on his warm pink cheek. ''Sorry, I must run, 'by, Uncle Phip—''

'By, Uncle Phip. A stinging at the back of her eyes. I have other things to do, Uncle Phip.

TWO

There was a surging terrifying roar from the engine as Vin, trying to pass an Exxon tank truck on a long hill, saw the car coming at them on the other side of the solid yellow center stripe, and pulled in ahead of the truck just, barely, in time.

"Vin!" Glenna cried. "Don't, please, fight any more of your battles with this car, with us in it—" She was white and shaking.

Timothy, in the back seat, said in his soft cool voice, "Would anyone like to join me in a good, final Act of Contrition? I think I remember it—'O my God, I am heartily sorry for having offended thee, and I detest all my sins because I dread the loss of heaven and the pains of hell—' "

"Shut up, Timothy," Vin said, but his shoulders shook with laughter. Most of his merriment had gone; but occasionally it bubbled up through the almost visible layers of worry, frustration, half-concealed rage and overhard living.

"It's not that I'm not grateful for the ride," Timothy said.

Vin, picking him up at that wretched crumbling brownstone on the Lower East Side, its broken pavements lined with battered stinking garbage cans, had thought to himself, Oh God, the starving artist descending from his garret, he'll embarrass the hell out of us, probably dirty and hairy and possibly drugged, but what can you do, he has no money and no other way to get up there, to North Truro. . . .

Timothy, gracefully managing a missing step coming down

from the high front door, surprised him pleasantly. Clean cream-colored suit, some kind of synthetic, on his long thin frame. The thick shining hair, like black satin, not hanging lower than his black eyebrows and not much longer than his earlobes, swinging around the high-cheekboned copper-colored face. The aquiline Converse cut of feature, in him, seemed to take on an almost Indian flavor, the look perhaps underscored by his having inherited bottomless sparkling dark eyes from his mother.

But then, he'd have to look halfway decent, at least part of the time. Vin was vaguely aware that he paid for his room and food and supplies, canvases, paint, brushes, by doing free-lance work in consumer research two or three days a week.

Anxious to get out of this ghastly neighborhood before some kid threw a rock and smashed a window of his Cadillac, Vin asked, "How's the art business, Timothy? Sold any paintings yet?"

He felt uncomfortable and out of place, talking about art. He had a feeling that artists, most of them, were queer, and while Timothy seemed all right, you never could tell.

"No," Timothy said. "Not yet. How's the armpit business?"

Vin flushed heavily at this reference to his profession, which was advertising.

Glenna said, "Look, you two, we have a three-hundred-mile drive ahead of us, let's pretend we're not related at all and be sweet and nice to each other."

Timothy thought she sounded abrasively gay and frightfully suburban. But then Vin, hounded-looking as he was, his bucket of success being emptied out if half-heard family rumors were true, must be difficult to live with. Someone, he supposed, had to pour oil. Not that he cared.

There was only one thing in the world he cared about.

Glenna swiveled around in her seat. "Poor lamb, you're too polite and correct, art or no art, to say that now you can go anywhere and paint anything. I can just see your great big airy studio—atelier—in Paris or Rome or Greece, the biggest tubes of the best oils . . . canvases stretched to order, huge ones . . . and then, after you're tired at your easel, wandering to a table of fruit and cheese and pouring wine into crystal. . . ."

Glenna had been an art major in college and had been thought promising, but Vin had snatched her and married her when she was twenty-three.

She sounded to Timothy remarkably like a patroness. He had had occasion to avoid several of these. *But you darling boy, what you want is a good square meal, and then . . .*

"Funny," Vin said, "that you're doing the proper traditional thing, going to join your family burying your uncle. Now that I think of it, I haven't seen you at a funeral for years. But of course"—as he took a corner too fast, heaving Glenna's hip against her door handle—"this is no ordinary funeral."

Although Marcia Converse Dalrymple did it the hard and most economical way—bus from New York to Providence, change for Hyannis, change again to a third bus for the down-Cape trip—she was, efficiently, the first to arrive at the house of mourning.

The bus let her out at the crossroads in North Truro, the last in the necklace of agreeable towns before the colorful explosion of Provincetown at the tip.

The house wasn't more than a half mile from the crossroads. It was an old and classically modest white Cape Cod cottage, misleading about the number and size of the rooms it held. Dark green shutters, kitchen ell to the right, climbing roses white-latticed across its clapboards. Sides and back of weathered salted shingles. An unassuming, slightly sunburned front lawn, an old herb garden and more lawn at the back with a gay rambling flower border looped around its perimeters—showing the hand of a casual and lighthearted gardener—under the pattering shade and sound of the aspens Phip had planted twenty-five years ago.

Right behind the border, the tawny moors began to lift themselves nakedly, fragrantly, to their great up and down sweep that halted itself in abrupt drama at cliff top, ninety feet give or take a few, over the Atlantic.

Turning in at the opening in the privet hedge, Marcia looked up into the catalpa and thought, Really, that tree is indecent.

Yes, an inconvenient place for her brother's death. She felt dusty and weary and burdened with every single hour of her sixty years. Her feet and ankles were swollen from the long hours on the bus.

And to think it could have been so comfortably, so handsomely done in the brownstone in New York, instead of at this faraway house dozing in the soft golden October sunlight, not looking at all like the residence of a man of great wealth.

Mrs. Grahn opened the dark green front door to Marcia's imperious single clang of the brass stirrup knocker.

Walking into the small square hall, from which the boxed-in staircase went upward recklessly steep, if short, Marcia gave a small instinctive and suspicious sniff. Over and above the scent of flowers she registered the smells of a house immaculately kept, wax, starch, the sweetness left behind by busy broom and mop and scrubbing brush.

While her nose inspected the housekeeper's efficiency, her eyes flickered over Mrs. Grahn. She had worked for Phip for the last two years since his dear Mrs. Trancey, incapacitated by arthritis, had had to retire. Mrs. Grahn did not fit Marcia's idea of how a woman in her position should look.

She was in her mid to late fifties, heavy-breasted, strong and straight. She had tightly crinkled red-gold hair, large pale blue eyes, red-rimmed now, and a bee-stung rosy mouth, the lips large and rounded, rimmed with a frill of flesh; somehow you couldn't immediately look away from them. No lipstick, she didn't need it. Her skin was so white as to be blue-veined at the temples. She wore a black shirtwaist dress which was unexceptionable but which seemed to make her hair burn redder and her skin whiter.

Marcia remembered with distaste that Sophie—really, Sophie's language!—invariably referred to her as Mrs. Groin.

"He's in the living room," Mrs. Grahn said, in her plummy voice.

To the left of the staircase was the dining room, to the right a little sunny sitting room-office. The living room, beyond these two rooms, ran the full width of the house. Behind that, at the back, was another long room that had once been a screened porch; Phip had had it converted into his library-bedroom when his heart forbade him to climb the steep flight of stairs to the bedroom floor above.

Marcia preceded Mrs. Grahn through the office and into the living room. The coffin was placed under two windows looking out into shaking aspen leaves. Leaf shadows trembled brightly and disturbingly over the dead man, suggesting life, movement.

Aware of being watched—surely the woman had some sense of propriety, surely she must know better?—Marcia said, "Leave me here, alone, please, Mrs. Grahn, with my brother."

Legs tired and stiff, she arranged herself on the velvet kneeler and studied Phip's face. Rosy, composed, thin, looking nothing like his seventy-two years; a flicker of sun fierily white in his thick hair.

She said her prayers for him, not taking very long about them. She felt it in extremely bad taste to make a display of oneself in this kind of final confrontation, even though now there was no one to see her.

Rising from the kneeler, she stood looking down. Shouldn't the shades be pulled to banish that quivering gay sunlight? There were no shades. Only the deep-ruffled starched white organdy curtains.

Phip was dressed in a fine gray wool suit, London-tailored, a white oxford cloth shirt, a paisley-patterned silk foulard tie in deep soft blues and greens. His—blanket, vulgar term, no doubt invented by florists, was small yellow rosebuds, white button chrysanthemums, and white and yellow marguerites.

What innocent-looking eyebrows he had, silky, straight-lined; what a singularly unmarked high forehead. Nothing here of the powerful man, of the unerring razored shrewdness that had guided him to his hauls of money. Nothing of the philandering Phip, Marica's word for him, who not very long ago was still amusing himself with women. And no doubt, she added tartly, wine and song.

The local people had been efficient enough. Everything seemed to be in order, although the black coffin looked, not to put too fine a point upon it, cheap. Tall candles burned in their stands at its head and foot. On a pewter tray on a nearby drop-leaf table, mass cards, notes of condolence, telegrams, were piling up.

Mrs. Grahn, with a light knock on the half-open door, came in carrying two immense ribbon-tied baskets. Already there were almost too many flowers: a glorious death garden of them, circling out in wings to fill a third of the long room.

There had been no funeral-parlor arranging of chairs. The room looked as Marcia remembered it from lazy summer visits. Glossy random-plank wooden floors painted sea blue, white walls, blue and white and fawn Chinese rugs, slightly faded gardeny chintzes and thin cool blue and white stripes slip-covering two love seats, a long down-cushioned sofa, and three comfortable low chairs. Books, a wall of them at the other end of the room, with the two windows framed attractively in the bookshelves. The fireplace scoured and empty, its brasses and bricks polished, two great white pots of ferns on either side of it.

When your back was turned to the coffin, and the flowers, all that was missing to make it completely normal was the music Phip liked to listen to, Mozart, Beethoven, with an occasional romp of New Orleans jazz; and the tinkle of ice in his glass of whiskey.

"I've put coffee and biscuits on a tray in the dining room for you," Mrs. Grahn said expressionlessly.

"Thank you. Let us have a word or so there as soon as you've placed the baskets."

The dining room was in restful shadow at this hour of the morning. Marcia seated herself at the large round faded mahogany table and poured coffee from a silver pot into a sprigged blue and white cup. She had a momentary feeling, bracing as brandy, of a house to run, to see to, servants to organize.

That had been a long time ago, the big house, her staff; before her husband Daniel had died. She had thought they were handsomely well off, and so had everybody else. He left her virtually penniless. Her home for the last ten years had been the three-room apartment, very dark, looking on an air well, but at an impeccable address in the East Sixties. Rent, food, clothing, cleaning woman, and her occasional austere enjoyments were paid for by Phip's monthly check.

("For God's sake, Marcia, why that address? You could have a nice bright little house somewhere for the gouger's rent they're charging you, a garden—"

("Are you suggesting Hempstead, Long Island—or perhaps

Yonkers? My friends would have no idea where to find me. My few remaining friends, that is, when the money goes your acquaintance narrows. . . . I'm afraid I never managed to acquire your bread-and-butter tastes.'')

Mrs. Grahn made her appearance. Marcia decided she hadn't been wrong in her first and barely recorded impression. There was a sort of sullenness and a concealed rage about the woman, like a banked fire.

Mrs. Grahn? ''Mrs.'' by marriage or courtesy? There was a ring on the proper finger.

Her mood was natural enough, in a way. The loss of a kind employer, a good undemanding job, board and lodging in two houses, a no doubt generous salary, although Phip would never say what he paid her.

''Now then, Mrs. Grahn,'' Marcia said, businesslike. ''What are the arrangements?''

''Arrangements? He's dead and he's going to be buried. If that's what you mean.''

Red spots flared on Marcia's high sharp cheekbones.

''I am referring to immediate practical matters. Accommodations, food—I think sit-down meals will not be necessary—''

''I should hope not!''

''—will not be necessary, Mrs. Grahn. But I think on both evenings a buffet, hot and cold foods—''

''I'd planned that anyway,'' with the strong implication that if she hadn't, Mrs. Daniel Dalrymple could whistle for her hot and cold buffets.

''Are the rooms all made up and ready?''

''Of course,'' Mrs. Grahn said in a manner Marcia described to herself as cheeky. ''The three rooms upstairs and the three over the garage. I don't think anyone would want to sleep in Mr. Converse's bed, in his room. Although naturally that's made up too, fresh.''

''We'll have to arrange to have some of the flowers taken to the hospital in Hyannis, at this rate the house won't hold them all. After, that is, their donors have come and gone. Perhaps Timothy, although I can't remember if he drives—''

The knocker sounded and, simultaneously, the telephone began what was to turn into its enraging unbreakable habit.

Out in the little hall, Sophie's drawl, Kate's rich soft voice, low.

The house, which had been for such a short time hers to command, was now invaded.

The white-painted garage, which had once been a modest barn, was across the road from the house. An old willow leaned over it. Sparrows nested in the rafters and splashed Phip's Land Rover with their droppings, but he would never let Mrs. Grahn broom the nests out. Whistling, he would clean off the birdlime with an old beach towel he kept on a hook in the garage.

Mr. Thomas Spiggott squatted under the willow tree, caressing with a light hand the leaves of a rare tender holly fern he had discovered, all but choked in the long grasses moving in the wind against the knotholed wood of the garage.

He had been watching, timidly putting his head out from behind the garage, for quite some time. First the tall thin figure of the hatted gray-haired woman, with her tired but forthright stride, turning in at the house. Later the florist's van. And now two young women arriving in a blue taxi from the airport.

For the fifth time, he said to himself, I wonder if I should . . .

And again answered himnself, No, a decent family funeral. Or anyway, not right now. Perhaps later. . . .

His conscience, however, bothered him badly. Not that it need amount to anything, his small niggling worry.

But Philip Converse had been so accommodating, so kind.

"Of course, Mr. Spiggott, do pursue your researches in the herb garden any hour of the day or night, I'd be interested myself to know what all those peculiar smells are. Will you take a glass of sherry before you get on with it?"

The herb garden went right up to the big back windows of Mr. Converse's library-bedroom.

THREE

"What *is* this?" Marcia asked rhetorically, with marked disapproval, of the person nearest her, who happened to be Kate. "A wake or a cocktail party?"

"There are certain resemblances . . ." Kate murmured, looking down at her glass.

The long living room was filled, people standing shoulder to shoulder. Smoke drifted in the sunlight, the acridity of tobacco putting up what was in a way a welcome fight with the drowning sweetness of the flowers.

The death notice inserted in the *Times* by Leo Converse had made it perfectly clear that Thursday was to be reserved for the family only; friends and associates could, if they wished, pay their respects on Friday. No one paid the slightest attention to these strictures.

There was, inevitably, and especially in Phip's house, subdued laughter and an occasional uninhibited loud seizure of it; the merriment increased with each foot of distance away from the coffin.

Favorite heart attack stories were told. "Aunt Augusta had just had her annual checkup, and he assured her, her man, Park Avenue, frightfully expensive, of course, that she was in perfect health, and she dropped dead on the sidewalk a block from his office. . . ."

"My nephew Al, suddenly at the eighteenth hole—sounds like a book, doesn't it? And not forty."

"We played croquet with him—with Phip—two days ago," a pretty, dark woman said to a heavy round woman. "And he was in marvelous shape. Caught John in front of the last two wickets before the post and swung his mallet and next thing you know John, or his ball, of course, was lodged, if you can believe it, fifty feet away in a fork of the willow tree across the street. . . ."

"Before you mention it," the heavy woman said, "yes, dear, I must go on a diet. . . ."

Behind her, Kate heard her cousin Vin saying to someone, in a low voice a fraction above a whisper and already a little blurred with gin, ". . . I mean, just take the minor bits and pieces, aside from the corporate properties. The house on Eighty-third Street, a quarter of a million, maybe. This place, peanuts, he only paid ten thousand for it, but"—a calculating pause—"that was roughly twenty-five years ago, and there are forty acres. And," on a long breath, "the paintings. Christ, the paintings."

Kate hadn't seen Vin for three or four months and was saddened and shocked when he came in and came over to her and hugged her.

He had always been a handsome man, thick dark hair, blue eyes, big bold features, high color; outgoing, jovial, brimming over with jokes and festivities; and assuming to himself the position of tolerant patriarch of their generation. He was forty-seven.

Now she saw, or sensed, the marks made by blows; the face of a man being battered about the head by life.

She suspected some of the reasons: living far beyond his means, although he made sixty-five thousand a year not counting bonuses and whatever company stock he might own.

Facing, at his agency, the onslaught of the young, in a business as ruthless about obsoletion as the manufacturers of automobiles; the open attempt, probably, to toss him on the garbage heap, after his shining climb to his vice-presidential summit.

Drinking too much, sleeping too little. A faint purpling under the skin, eyes too bright, flesh losing its tight fit under them.

And his children: "How's the family, Vin, the kids?"

"Rotten as everybody else's." His voice loud and cheerful. "One college dropout, one unmarried mother, one bad trip. Don't tell *me* I'm not in the swim."

She was very fond of him and knew that he was of her.

"Where are you up to now, Kate, twenty-nine thousand? A thousand for every year of your life—well, keep it up, love, lap it up while you may. You're too modest and retiring is what's wrong with you, there's a girl at our place twenty-three who's making thirty—"

Vin had gotten her her first job in advertising; the copy chief was a friend of his. She knew that she could have done it on her own; there were a lot of things about herself she wasn't sure about, but her own facile talent was never in question.

Vin, though, had made it easy and swift, had said, "You want a blue-chip place where you can dive headfirst into television, none of this backstairs beginners' crap."

Glenna behind him, smiling over his shoulder at Kate. Lithe and tanned, vigorous, suggesting the open air, club terraces, station wagons, and golf carts. But now with a tension on her attractive thin brown face, a weariness behind her eyes. Vin, of course.

"You look good, Glenna," Kate heard a man who was a stranger to her say. And Glenna's answer, her laugh a little hard-edged. "God—the battle—the hair coloring, the diet, I'm cottage-cheesed half to death—forty lengths in the pool every day and three sets of tennis, vats of stay-young cream, I would love, I would adore, to be a slob. *What* a rest. . . ."

Timothy stood alone in a corner near the dining room door.

Kate wondered if she should go over and talk to him but then decided she wouldn't. When he had first come in, he had greeted her with, "How's the lady executive?" which she found anything but flattering, if not openly, smilingly hostile.

Sophie overheard him and said, irritated on Kate's behalf, "Well, we can't all be aspirin' but so far unsung artists, can we now, Timothy honey, and you must admit she looks more like a deer that just ambled out of the forest than any old executive. . . ."

Jack Converse arrived. In chalk-striped dark blue, tall, vivid, his expressive face like a mirror, grave now, intent; but unknowingly bringing with him into this room of death a relish in life, a sense of strong motion like a gust of wind.

Kate watched him walk to the coffin, kneel, study Phip with bent head; he was there for perhaps three minutes. His silent presence sent almost visible waves through the room.

He got up from the kneeler, stood quietly, lost in something for the moment—Phip, himself, the two of them?—and then with a brisk backhanded movement dealt with his tears.

"Well," Sophie said softly, having allowed him his privacy, "if it isn't the First Prize."

He came over and gave her a great fond hug and kiss. "Hello, Sophie, you swamp rat," he said, and looked over her golden head at Kate.

His eyes were a distillation of all the Converse blues: the purest essence of blue, set deep and brilliant under heavy comely black eyebrows. A number of generations of handsome people before him had contributed the raking bone structure; but the vibrating kind of style and being, the lively throwaway grace, were things of his own.

"Kate," he said. "And how are you, Kate?"

She had a sensation of a sudden jar, and the ground shifting under her feet. The earth, she thought frivolously, just took a very sharp turn. One is so seldom aware that one is on a ball spinning in space.

But, more sensibly explained, the early start to the day, too much coffee, two airline terminals, Kennedy and Logan with their endless echoing passages, two plane flights, the whack over the heart at seeing that it was really true, that Phip was really dead. To say nothing of midday scotch and only the smallest attempt at food, a cracker with some cheese on it, half a cucumber sandwich, and three cherry tomatoes.

"I'm all right, Jack," she said and laughed a little and added, "How many times a week do you have to listen to that particular statement?"

He put an arm lightly about her shoulders and kissed her temple, an embrace that seemed to her to establish them again, quite comfortably, as cousins.

But, his face that close, she thought how endearing the wet stuck-together dark lashes were; and was pleased that he was

an open man, capable of tears. The other male Converses had
so far been stiff-upper-lipped at the loss of Phip.

"You crackled at me," Jack said with interest. "Carpet
electricity, I suppose. I keep forgetting what a nice girl you
are, Kate, it's too bad we only meet at weddings and funerals."

The telephone rang. Sophie, nearest it, picked it up and
listened and handed it to Kate.

"Vasco da Gama."

"Who?" Jack asked.

"Well, properly, Ferdie di Castro. Kate's Latin lover, or
one of them. As far as I know, no kin to the Cuban chap."
Turning her head to the window at the slam of a car door, "By
the prickin' of my thumbs, someone prominent this way comes.
Yes, the United States Senate, in person."

Like everybody else entering the room, Garrett Converse
went immediately to the coffin and knelt; but Kate felt an
invisible aura of brass bands, flags, hot television lights, and
whirring cameras. He was a personable and controversial figure,
alternately accused of being too liberal veering on Red, and
too middle-of-the-road, depending on what party you belonged
to; too honest, too witty, too plausible, too geared to money
and power, too devoted to the interests of minorities.

Commandingly tall and just verging on portly, with a finely
sculpted head of shining white hair, the bold aquiline Converse
nose, fair immaculately shaven skin, and a piercing blue gaze
under alert hooked dark eyebrows, he looked the very picture
of a senator.

He rose and scanned the room, spotted Jack, and came over
to the group of three by the window, nodding, smiling, pausing
for a word here, a word there, a handshake, on the way.

When he got close, Kate wondered what was wrong with
him, something gray under the pink of his skin, something odd
about the blue eyes. Grief, overwork, a hangover, and possibly
all three. He wore a superb dark charcoal suit, a white shirt,
and a glossy black silk necktie, splendidly windsor-knotted.

"Hello, Senator," Jack said. "Did I ever tell you you dress
like a Republican?"

Garrett studied his nephew's chalk tripes, vested, and said,

"So do you, Jack, come to think of it. Sophie dear, Kate dear."
Quick kisses.

Perhaps I'm going around the bend, Kate thought, everybody
seems different, unfamiliar, first Jack and now her Uncle Garrett. She felt something coming from him, something like fear,
or like a hole in the wall of his confidence.

Garrett was watching Jack's face as though the features were
entirely new to him.

In a voice that had nothing to do with the intensity of his
gaze, he said, "It's only at family ceremonies I can afford to
be seen publicly with Jack. Otherwise I would be immediately
tagged as Informed Source or Unimpeachable Authority—Jack,
you're empty, come help me find a drink."

The rich, rounded voice was polished with years of addressing large attentive audiences.

In the dining room, the long mahogany buffet held the funeral
liquids. Marcia had been taken aback and Jack amused at the
Bacchanalian look of the arrangement, one dozen bottles of
everything, scotch, rye, brandy, gin, vodka, vermouth, Bourbon, rum, Irish whiskey. Beer and champagne bottles sunk in
ice, trays of glasses glittering now that the sun had moved from
the zenith a little to the west.

"*Really,*" Marcia had said to Leo Converse. "I hardly think
this is quite—"

"Phip's orders," Leo said.

The display reminded Jack of one of his cherished Phip
stories. At his age inevitably a frequent attender at other
people's funerals, Phip had upon the demise of someone named
Schmidt suffered through an hour-long requiem mass, taken
up his duties, at the request of the family, as a pallbearer ("I
swear to God, Jack, the fellow wasn't in there at all, the coffin
was full of paving stones, it was that heavy"), and gone to the
cemetery and back in a March hailstorm. When at last he
reached the haven of the Schmidt town house, and warmth,
and rest, and food and drink, a Schmidt nephew had asked in
a hushed voice, "What can I get you, Mr. Converse?" "Well
now . . ." A thirsty hesitation. "We have everything, Mr.
Converse. You name it, we have it. Ginger ale, 7-Up, Sprite,

Coca-Cola, orange pop, lemonade, chocolate milk, and oh yes, lots of hot coffee. And cocoa." Phip, eyes almost starting out of his head, had suddenly remembered a business appointment. Someone with a pier for sale, on the Hudson River.

Garrett helped himself to a large scotch. His hands were a little shaky, uncharacteristic of them.

He raised his glass toward the window, saluting the blue sky outside. "God rest you, Phip."

And then said, very carefully and warily to Jack, "Well—what's new?"

Before his nephew could frame an answer, there was a sudden growing, descending roar. The house seemed to tremble. Bottles rattled against each other and glasses uttered crystal sounds.

Jack could feel his lips moving but couldn't hear what they said. Garrett turned white and reached for his heart.

What might, in the appalling din, be a man's shout—Vin's?—and a woman's scream suggested themselves from the living room.

Jack ran out into the hall and through the open front door in time to see the glittering silver of the four-seater plane lift itself from perhaps fifty feet over the chimney, poke its nose sharply upward, and swing northwest, probably bound for the Provincetown airport.

Into the stunned and terrified silence Sophie said on a long gasping breath, "Three guesses, everyone, about who just buzzed this house. It wasn't the angels come to get Phip. For my money, it was someone transportin' Tike to the obsequies."

Nobody argued with her conclusion. Handkerchiefs wiped blanched and sweating faces. Tike Converse was variously cursed, damned, and blasted, up and down the length of the room.

Timothy glanced thoughtfully at his father.

Leo looked grim, but that was not at all unusual for him.

He was an immensely tall, thin man, six feet four or five inches, with a long gloomy saturnine face seamed with deep vertical wrinkles. His nose was large, long, and beaked. His sunken blue eyes, dragged down at the lower lids like a hound's, had an expression, always, of expecting the worst, of things and people. His hair had remained dark and rose in an untidy thatch above his high frown-marked forehead. When he spoke, his voice seemed to come up from some deep echoing dark cavern.

"I'd much rather," Phip had been heard to say, "have a pessimist for a lawyer than an optimist."

Jack had taken occasion to murmur to Kate a while back, "Look at him, *The Anatomy of Melancholy*, large as life, an ideal mourner, wouldn't you say?"

Leo went to his sister Marcia. She was alarmingly white around the mouth, trembling, and obviously close to fainting. With a rusted-over kind of gentleness, he said, "Here . . . the sofa . . . one dead body in this room is more than enough. Timothy, get some brandy and hurry."

Sophie had been correct in her assumption. Tike arrived twenty minutes later. She walked in smiling and holding her head high, as though daring anyone to scold her.

"Congratulations, Tike," Timothy said, not loudly, but somehow everyone in the room heard him. "From the point of view of any heart patients here, and there must be at least a few, you scored a direct hit."

"It wasn't my fault," Tike said defiantly. "I only thought I saw the roof of the house and showed him, and he dove. Just like that."

Phip in his coffin caught her eye and she stared with astonished distaste. Then, off balance, uncertain, she walked over and went down awkwardly on one knee.

"Fat lot of good three years in a convent school did that one," Sophie said to Kate. "She's probably countin' up to ten till it's decent to rise and shine again. If you call that shinin'."

Tike was dressed head to foot in secondhand 1940s clothes, a limp flowered dark blue dress with the hem dangling at mid-shin, thick pinkish rayon stockings seamed at the back, red ankle-strapped platform-soled shoes, and a terrible small hat of red straw, tipped over her forehead, holding her hair behind in a crocheted pink snood.

From across the room her father said in his harsh cavernous voice, "Good afternoon, Angela."

Jack caught something in the voice, and the use of her given name. The dents of mirth, of living, near his mouth corners deepened as Kate watched.

Timothy said driftingly, as though he was thinking about something else, "All that money, Tike—you're smeared over even my poor man's drugstore, with your face glaring at me from somebody's plastic cosmetics stand—how come you could take the time off to come here and bring the house down?"

"I just thought I'd join you all, standin' in line at the teller's winda," Tike said, in a crude imitation of Sophie's accent.

Sophie looked at her, for a moment seeming a good deal older, and pale, and raging.

Bad taste, the roomful of people said silently; but a number of them unconnected by blood with the family were delighted.

Frightful as her clothing was, Tike held the eye. Not pretty, not beautiful. There were a lot of enchanting girls around, but they didn't make a hundred dollars an hour, minimum rate. Or not, at least, in front of a camera.

A fad face, fitting her own time. Heart-shaped, coming down to a chin with a deep dimple in the middle of it, a chocolate-box joke on everybody. The face pointedly blank, deliberately unknowing, unfeeling. Amber hair cut in short petals around her small head. Half-moon eyelids holding her amazing spike-lashed purple-blue eyes—"with the expression, dear Tike, of a depraved *baby*," the photographer Loren MacLaren said to her. Thin recklessly tilted upper lip over the natural full pout of the lower lip. Five feet nine, meltingly slender in motion and hard as a rock in bone and muscle and spine.

And above and beyond her physical appearance, a flash and flare and a dangerous unspoken "I'm me and I'm great, and whoever you are get out of my way. Or else."

In the mysterious manner of wakes, the room in a short time emptied itself, except for the family and one little elderly woman with a sad, snub, bulldog face, who someone said had been Phip's secretary years ago.

The emptying was fortunate; because at a little before three o'clock Mrs. Stella Grahn made her entrance.

FOUR

Until now her presence in the house had been noticeable only in connection with services and conveniences: ice buckets re-filled, trays of sandwiches placed on the dining room table, ashtrays emptied, kitchen sounds of things being washed up.

She had changed her black shirtwaist dress for a black silk, with a cameo brooch at the throat, and her sensible black shoes for high-heeled pumps. There was about her the air of a woman bathed, brushed, perfumed, for an important occasion.

No one paid her any particular attention as she went and knelt by the coffin.

Perhaps it was a low laugh from a far corner of the room, Sophie and Jack together, that triggered her.

She rose from the kneeler and turned and faced the room.

"Laugh you may, with him lying there and all his worldly goods to split up among you"—the voice kiting high with fury.

"Mrs. Grahn!" icily, from Marcia, with the unspoken, Remember your place, Mrs. Grahn.

A sort of spasm passed over Mrs. Grahn's face.

She cried out, "He didn't die of his heart, he was killed, murdered in his bed," the words tumbling over each other now, the voice even higher, "and it has to be one of you, here, he hadn't an enemy in the world, everybody loved him—"

Color surged under her white skin. The pale blue eyes seemed to have an unearthly accusing shine.

A quiet voice near her—Jack had moved away from his

27

corner—asked, "But why, Mrs. Grahn? Why do you say that?"

"Because he was going to marry me."

Triumphant, shoulders squared. She was breathing hard.

"The woman's been drinking," Marcia said to Leo.

"—Yes, marry me. That's right, stare. Mr. Philip Andrew Converse marrying his housekeeper? Well, I want to tell you I went to school like everybody else, and a good and respectable man—Mr. Grahn—wanted me and married me and died a *natural* death, and I hold that running two houses and seeing to every wish and whim of Mr. Converse's and making him happy and comfortable and providing him with the food he likes and that doesn't give him indigestion is a life for a woman to be proud of and not apologize for. . . ."

Tears began to thicken her voice. "I was right at his side when he called Mr. Leo Converse—he told me that he'd left me a nice little annuity, but in view of the fact that I'd be Mrs. Philip Converse there'd of course be changes, and Mr. Leo Converse was out of town, on a case, in Albany. But someone heard about it, someone killed him, someone right here murdered him in his bed—"

A great pour of tears overtook her. She bent almost double, clasping herself as though in physical pain.

Then she straightened and screamed, "But God will judge, God will punish, God will find out and let everybody know, *Thou shalt not kill,*" and turned and walked weeping from the room.

She left behind her a profound silence.

Kate for the first time in this room could hear the ticking of the French porcelain clock, painted with violets, on the mantelpiece.

Aspen leaves lightly tickled the window screen beyond Phip; someone had opened the windows before Mrs. Grahn's entrance, to clear the room of smoke, and a clean salty breeze went past her cheek.

A sneeze broke the silence, a curiously reassuring, normal, human sound.

Glenna looked around her, and explained, "Hay fever." And added, "God bless me, as nobody else will."

"Drinking, or mad, or both," Marcia said. "I always thought

she was a most unsuitable sort of woman for the job.''

"Love is bustin' out all over,'' Sophie said. Her eyes were narrowed. ''I agree with you in ways, Marcia, a touch of the whore, but I never heard of *that* puttin' a woman out of the great race. And she does combine it with God this, and God that, sort of balances out the size-forty bosom in a way—''

"For Christ's sake, Sophie!'' Vin's face had gone a thunderous red. ''Do you always have to be funny?''

"Well, if I can't laugh at my own funeral, I feel free to indulge at darlin' Phip's.''

"Of course,'' Garrett said. ''Of course, Sophie. Sane Sophie. Ridiculous, all of it, but unpleasant. . . .''

He had started out rather shakily, but his voice rolled richly into confidence as it struck his own ears. ''Overcome, poor lady. Grief, shock—it takes us all in strange ways.''

Tike giggled explosively. ''What a joke, if it was true, but an old *man*, how could he, *you* know.'' She put a finger to the tipped-down brim of her awful hat and went on, ''Not that I . . . I mean, I made nine thousand five hundred dollars last month, or maybe it took me six weeks to earn it. . . .''

"Don't bother countin' your money in public,'' Sophie said. ''Anyone can tell you're rich from the way you're dressed, Tike.''

"I must go,'' the little woman with the bulldog face said. Everyone had forgotten she was there.

"And naturally . . .'' She paused in the doorway. ''Naturally, I won't say anything, don't anyone worry,'' and was gone.

"She'll only dine out on it for the rest of her life,'' Timothy murmured. ''Did anyone get her name?''

"Dorothea something. Go check the guest book.'' Leo's first words in some time. The vertical seams of his face had if possible deepened.

Kate looked over, for comfort and enlightenment, at Jack's face, usually so vividly readable.

It wasn't, at the moment. He looked pale, and she thought she felt his shock.

But perhaps she was only projecting her own feeling of shock; the inner trembling, not surprising after the doomy plunge of the plane over the house, the feeling of obliteration

approaching, and just now the Roman-candle eruption of Mrs.
Grahn, in tears and rage and accusation, and the two words
that didn't come easily to the mind, or tongue, no matter how
often you read them, heard them, newspapers, radio, television.

Killed. Murdered.

"Is everything satisfactory?"

A hushed male voice from the dining room door; a young
man with a raw pink face, in a dismally black suit, gray leather
gloves on his hands.

The entire room glared at him.

"Verney's," he said, sounding taken aback. "In charge of
the arrangements for Mr. Converse. They told me to come and
ask, Is everything satisfactory?"

"The undertakers," Leo said, as if the young man wasn't
there. "Yes, yes—leave us if you will."

Silence again.

Then Jack said, "Someone has to talk to her. We can't leave
this thing hanging in midair."

"*Talk* to her!" Vin started out softly enough. "What?—give
credence to the woman's ravings? Tell her, Yes, we take you
seriously indeed, Mrs. Grahn, perhaps Mr. Philip Converse
was murdered by one of his relatives to keep him from marrying
you, with the resulting possible loss of funds, some of it or all
of it—"

His voice mounted in volume with his rage.

"Our hero, the seeker after truth and the hell with everything
and everybody else, screw them all"—inserting an attempt at
a sorrowful chant—"when my poor daddy went down in his
B-26 in the English Channel and I was only six months old,
dear Uncle Phip took over and put me through school and
college in the style to which I feel I am naturally born. . . ."

He paused to take a furious swallow of his drink.

Glenna, white, touched his arm. "Vin—"

Old jealousies surfaced in Vin's voice and on his clenched,
flaming face. "Will you have a sailboat, my poor fatherless
Jack? A year at the Sorbonne, Jack? Nothing's too good for
you, Jack my boy. Yes, you won't sit idly by now, will you—
you bloody interfering housewrecking son of a bitch—"

Jack went over to him and snatched him to his feet. Marcia

almost threw her tall thin body between them, crying, "He, dead there, and the two of you desecrating the air with your fighting and cursing— Sit down, both of you, at once."

"Yes, Nanny," Jack said, looking as though he had immediately rescued his control; Kate saw him glance over at the coffin before he obediently sat down.

Vin stayed defiantly on his feet, swaying a little, fury or drink or both, Kate thought.

A light cool voice from behind her, Timothy's, observed. "Newspaperman found dead at foot of Atlantic bluffs. Police concluded that John Converse in his grief over his deceased uncle had emptied a bottle and taken a night walk and failed to see the edge of the hundred-foot drop near Highland Light, in North Truro. . . ."

Sounding pleased with himself, he continued, "Converse fortune in deadlock, long and costly litigation foreseen, the notable Converse collection will remain under lock and key for years even though avid dealers and private collectors are—"

Before she could stop herself, Kate turned her head and looked up into Timothy's dark sparkling eyes and said, "Are you really heartless, Timothy, or do you just sound that way?"

A faint color came up under his copper skin. He jingled coins in the pocket of his trousers.

"Another county heard from," he said.

Jack looked consideringly over at her. She was in appearance pleasantly out of place among the Converses. In this light, a skin of rose, faint green, and olive. Tipped-up eyes, long, golden, vulnerable; cloudy dark shining hair wrapped around her head and folded under at the back; a long neck. Not in any way a contemporary face, the gypsy coloring in odd contrast with the deer's eyes. Fine slender body, graceful; dressed quietly but not mournfully in a thin gray wool suit which, tailored to an edge, pearl-buttoned and pleated, looking thoroughly female on her.

Another county indeed. A Spanish grandmother, if he remembered correctly, and some French blood; but a dose of Irish, too, her surname had been O'Donough before it was legally changed to Converse when his Uncle Hugh and Aunt Livia had adopted her.

Vin half sat, half collapsed on the flowery down-cushioned sofa.

"Well then," he said in a drained voice, "do we all understand each other?"

Jack's eyes went to Sophie's face.

"Sophie?" Fondness, but with an observing and acute question mark.

She hesitated, and then, not looking at him but fixedly at one of the white pots of fern on the rosy brick hearth, said, "How many handsome houses have you seen, the windows all boarded up, no one enjoyin' the palatial grounds and garden, and you wonder why, and ask, and you're told, The place is in litigation? Years go by and the boards are still up. I can see it now, suits and countersuits. And then appeals. You don't go interitin' money if you kill to get it. But did anyone? And how will it ever come to light?—not," she seemed to be saying to herself sharply, "that I believe that woman's romantic ramblin's. Meantime, the lawyers linin' their pockets, dippin' into the estate like a great big pot of honey—oh sorry, Leo. . . ."

"Think nothing of it," Leo said. "Replacing the *g*'s, you have just spoken my mind, Sophie." He leaned, dark, towering, his face a mask of gloom, against the bookshelves.

Bending forward in his chair, long back, strong hands locked between his knees, Jack moved his blue eyes from face to face. He was alight with an objective and unrepentant curiosity and concern.

"Kate?" he asked.

Kate's eyes fell on Marcia's face, stripped suddenly to the bones. Grief at her brother's death? Shock at the reverberations in his house, of doom and naked rage? She remembered Sophie's telling her Marcia was probably completely dependent on Phip.

And Vin, sprawled on the sofa, bruised with his own outburst, kind jovial battered Vin—

"Are you up here covering, or shall we say creating, a story? Or are you buying an uncle who was extremely good to everybody and especially, very especially, to you, Jack?" Garrett Converse said. His voice was calm.

Jack looked at him, said, "Answer your own question to

your own taste, Senator,'' looked back at Kate and spoke her name, lightly and crisply, again.

She said, "I pass," and was surprised at the breathlessness of her voice, and immediately ashamed and wretched.

What she had wanted to say was, I don't really see what else you can do, Jack, than ask her, pin it down, one way or another, better or worse.

There was a long pause.

"Well," Jack said, getting to his feet, "as I said before Vin so rudely interrupted me, somebody's got to talk to that woman. If you think she's going to leave it at this, you're crazy."

Vin walked hurriedly past him, bent a little as if in pain, obviously on his way to the upstairs bathroom to be sick.

"Jack, you can't seriously believe—" Glenna began harshly, her eyes following Vin.

"Why not?" Jack asked. "Old and lonely. Death staring him in the face. He's never had anyone of his own, just relatives to borrow. When they could—especially me, as Garrett said in another connection—spare him the time. After all, she was already performing most of the functions of an admirable wife, clean houses, good food, company, and all the care he could use— "

His voice was hard and ringing.

There was a heavy authoritative knock at the half-open front door, and the sound of footsteps that made the blue-painted random-plank floors faintly tremble.

A tall stout man paused in the doorway a foot or so away from Jack.

"Police Chief Dutra, Provincetown," he said. Extending a huge amiable hand to the other man's, "Peter Dutra."

FIVE

Glenna sneezed and said faintly, "Well. God bless me again."

Sophie knocked over her empty champagne glass. It smashed itself to pieces, delicately and musically.

"Promise me," Phip had said, long ago, knowing her fondness for this beverage, "you'll drink champagne at my funeral."

"I do most faithfully promise, Uncle Phip. And if—the rag trade bein' what it is—I predecease you, a vat of scotch for you, at mine."

In a gesture that looked at once powerful and protective, Leo folded his arms across his chest.

"Good afternoon, Chief," Jack said.

There was a fearful crash from the hall, an explosive "Almighty God—"

The sounds explained themselves all too clearly to the family. Vin must have missed his footing on the steep little dangerous staircase; fortunately, it turned out, only three steps from the bottom. Kate wondered if the official voice in the doorway had knocked him off balance.

Jack went to his aid, accompanied by an alert and curious Dutra. He was sprawling on hands and knees, shaking his head as though he couldn't believe he wasn't living in a bad dream.

He said, "Take your hands off me."

"Darling," Glenna in the doorway cried and ran and helped

him to his feet. She turned and said to everyone, anyone, "Excuse us. I'm going to see him into his bed for a nap. Starting off as we did so early, and that awful drive—he's utterly exhausted. . . ."

As they reassembled in the living room, " 'Exhausted' is a new word for it," Marcia said in an acid but mechanical fashion, an automatic knuckle-rapping; she was staring at Dutra.

With desperate authority, she announced to him, "And about this visit of yours, it's preposterous, the whole thing, absolute and utter nonsense."

Police Chief Dutra looked back at her out of warm brown eyes.

"Well, it happens," he said.

Watched with enormous attention, he went and knelt down by Phip's coffin, and remained there for two minutes that seemed twenty.

"I thought," Timothy said later, "that he was saying the whole Litany of the Saints to himself."

Dutra finally rose from his knees and looked questioningly around as if waiting for something.

Jack grasped blindly for a straw and found it.

"Food and drink in the next room, Chief Dutra."

"Ah." Large hands were rubbed together, his unspoken request obviously answered.

"I wouldn't mind a drop. Shakes you up. It happens, as I said to this good lady. Fine fellow. Many's the drink we shared in life," and then, looking startled, "in his, I mean, when *he* was alive," thus rising out of the grave he had just verbally dug for himself.

Jack led him to the drinks table in the dining room. They both listened to the sound of footsteps, Vin's and Glenna's, crossing the little hall and going out the door, Vin saying in a blurred way, "That policeman—what was he—?" and Glenna's "Sssshhh."

Dutra gave Jack a portentous wink, as he lifted his large glass of ginger ale and bourbon.

"Overcome," he said. "Who's to blame him? I remember when my mother . . ."

Jack propped himself patiently against the table and heard all about the long illness and lingering death of Police Chief Dutra's mother.

We all look, Kate thought, as though we're waiting to be summoned to the dentist's chair.

After a time, the voice in the dining room stopped, the front door closed firmly, and Jack came back to the living room. He went over to Kate and took her wrist and drew her to her feet.

"Come with me, Kate. I need a witness—another county, as Timothy said after he had disposed of me over the edge of the cliff—and in case she has hysterics I may need a womanly hand."

"Jack, I forbid this," Marcia said.

"I am thirty-two, Aunt Marcia, not seven, and you haven't just caught me stealing a dime from your change purse. It has to be done, that's all there is to it, you can't just look the other way."

There was a closed door at the end of the coffin nearest the fireplace wall that led to the kitchen wing. The kitchen was empty. It was a big comfortable sitting kitchen with cream and red toile curtains, the blue wooden floors spatter-dashed to match, a round oak table blanched with scrubbing, a gingham-cushioned rocker near one window, an old black coal stove like a monument, lovingly polished, with a shining electric one across the room from it, a loudly ticking wall clock, and a black cat curled in a pane-patterned oblong of sun.

There were signs that its proprietress was not far away. A scent of baking bread from the oven of the black stove, something simmering in a heavy red enameled French pot on one of its burners, salad makings on the counter beside the sink, a cake cooling on a rack.

"Well, her cooking smells authentic, anyway," Jack said.

The kitchen had a door opening on the front lawn and another in the opposite wall, leading to the back yard. Under the largest of the aspen trees was a lacy white wrought-iron settee flanked with chairs. Mrs. Grahn was sitting there, in her black dress. There was a round white iron table in front of her with a bowl of fruit on it. She was slowly eating grapes. Her face was stained with tears.

She made as if to get up and Jack said, "Relax, Mrs. Grahn. Do you feel able to talk, a little?" His voice was neither friendly nor unfriendly.

"Yes."

He deliberately asked, first, the hardest and most dangerous question for him to utter.

"If you think Uncle Phip was killed, why didn't you go right to the police?"

"I didn't want to disgrace him—his family—drag him into the headlines," Mrs. Grahn said. "I first thought, What's done's done. And then when I thought more about it—"

"About his being as you say on the brink of marrying you, and wanting to change his will? And then it seemed that what was just a vague impression of yours was true—actual fact?"

"It wasn't just a vague impression," Mrs. Grahn said hotly. "I left him well and happy, sitting up in his bed playing solitaire. He always insisted I have my weekly night off, as well as my Sundays, to visit my sister and friends in Provincetown, he refused to be made an invalid. . . ."

Jack was half sitting on the table; Kate was in one of the white chairs. Floating light and shade webbed them, found the blue veins at Mrs. Grahn's temples, and twinkled on the plump red lips with their frill of flesh.

"Playing solitaire, like I said. His color was good. He'd had his bath, and his nightcap was on the table beside him, one ounce of whiskey in a tall glass, the rest water. He said, 'Enjoy yourself, Stella, let 'er rip. Don't lose too much money playing pinochle, I think that sister of yours has a pack of marked cards.' "

Well. Death could take a man of seventy-two, bathed and with his drink at his elbow, slapping down his kings and queens and aces on his walnut bed table. If natural, a well-deserved quick end for Phip. How much better to think of it that way, leave it that way—

But.

"I came home later than usual," Mrs. Grahn said, looking

not at them but into some dark place. "I accuse myself of that, I might have been able to stop whoever it was, murdering him."

A thin cold shiver rippled over Kate's skin in the warm gold of the afternoon.

"And you found him, when, how—" Jack was pale and intent.

"I drove home in my car a little after one, I'd gotten caught up in the game. I put the car in the garage and let myself in at the front kitchen door with my key—the door was locked, but all of them"—she gestured at the house—"could have keys, the way they come and go here, when it's summer, and vacation time, and convenient to come to swim and sail and sunbathe, and get a free room and food while they're paying their respects to their uncle. . . ."

In a steering way, Jack said, "Yes, you let yourself in, and?"

"I felt guilty about being late. I wanted to see that he was comfortably asleep and did he need an extra blanket, the night had turned very chilly. The quiet of the room worried me but I didn't want to startle him awake by turning on the light, and when my eyes got adjusted I saw he was spilled in a way, sideways, half off his pillows, and the bed tray was on the floor, and cards scattered every which way—and I turned on the light—"

She covered her face with her hands.

"He was dead," she said into her palms, "and looking at me, looking right at me, dead, no pulse, no heartbeat, the bedclothes all roiled and thrashed around, I tidied them to make the bed more comfortable. . . ."

Kate got up and walked away from her voice. Jack would have to do without his witness.

She stood looking down at Phip's herbaceous border. Now, in October, still blossoming merrily. Mounds of white sweet alyssum, chrysanthemums, bronze and frosty pink and mauve, yellow and white. A few late zinnias, lavender cosmos floating in the light wind, roses making a last fragrant flare of salmon and gold and pink-flushed ivory.

She could hear the flat voice, going on; but not what was being said.

"It took a long time to track down Dr. Littauer, Mr. Converse's doctor up here, his answering service said where he was, a party, I suppose—but it turned out they'd all gone on to another party. I had to call the police and they found him somehow or other and he came out here about ten-thirty and spent about ten minutes with Mr. Converse.''

He got her implication clearly: the doctor having been partying, drinking, the hasty examination before the signing of the death certificate.

"Mrs. Grahn," Jack said carefully, "if, every time an elderly and often ill patient died, his doctor ran around in circles shouting foul play, police, murder, autopsy, things would pretty well clank to a halt.''

"I know him," she said stubbornly. "Every line, every tint of Mr. Converse's face, every mood. He was well. He was hale. He was healthy—''

This, Jack thought, could go on endlessly. Hale. Well. I *know*.

"Have you anything, by the way, in writing? About your claim that he wanted to marry you?''

"Writing! Why would he write to me, the two of us together all the time—and if I did, do you think I'd give it to you to burn or destroy or tear up? No. I have nothing in writing. I have nothing,'' Mrs. Grahn said into the hands again cupping her face, "at all, now.''

Full stories are never extracted from people by hewing to delicacy and good manners, however much the questioner may wish to retreat to them.

"How do you suppose any of the family might have heard of this . . . proposed alliance? I didn't. And I was probably the closest of us to him.''

"Did you ever hear of the word 'gossip,' Mr. Converse?''

"And what are your plans now?''

"Plans? Well, Mr. Leo Converse asked me to stay here at the house until after the funeral to see to things. . . .''

And to watch, and listen, and accuse, and watch some more, he thought; otherwise she might have flatly refused to make beds and cook and provide ice and clean ashtrays for a murderer.

"And then what?''

"You're not asking me where or how I'll live or how I'll

get along without Mr. Philip Converse?''

"No, I'm not."

"I don't know." Mrs. Grahn stared at a wasp that had just lighted on an apple in the fruit bowl, and then gave her hand a shooing wave. "Those things can kill you, wasps, I mean, if they get you in the right place, near the eye, they say—I don't know. Perhaps the good God will decide the matter for me one way or another. And for you, all of you. . . . Now, if you'll pardon me, I have to get back to my bread. And my salad. Mouths to feed. Regardless."

There was a light hand on Kate's shoulder and she was surprised to feel the comfort in it.

And was startled to feel the surprise in the hand itself, a tightening over her flesh and bone, a lingering, and then a gentle withdrawal that was, almost, a stroking motion, down one of her shoulder blades.

"Sorry, Kate. And thank you. . . ."

She turned to face this magnetic stranger, this cousin. Enjoy him, as Sophie did. The First Prize. In the near presence of death, count your blessings, nice people, warmth, comfort, affection.

"I'm the one to be sorry . . . a coward . . . but those thrashed-about bedclothes, it was all too . . ."

"I know."

"And . . . what?"

Understanding the one-word question, he said, "Nothing at all to go on, really. It may be that she just wanted him, so badly, to live—and not necessarily for selfish or financial reasons—that she's sure someone deliberately flouted her. To say nothing of *him*."

Almost to himself, he said, "His one drink, I've known him to cheat, and dip into the bottle, and his sleeping pill on top of that—"

He looked over her head at the lifting moors, his voice strange, seeming to come from a long way away. " 'Flouting' would hardly be the word, if someone near and dear came at you in the dark . . . and you were dazed and only half functioning and not sure whether it was a bad nightmare, or real . . . and picked up, say, a pillow and you saw it coming at your head, to smother you, he wasn't shot and presumably not poisoned, although probably in her neat way she washed out his glass just as she tidied his bed to make him more comfortable—''

''*Jack!*''

''And the undertakers would tidily powder over any developing bruises of a death throe. . . .''

He shook his head a little; reminiscent of Vin in a way, sadly and ludicrously on his hands and knees in the hall.

''Jack!'' Another voice, commanding, from the screen door of the kitchen. Marcia came out.

''Leo and Garrett have gone off somewhere; Vin is, I presume, asleep; Tike has just lit a cigarette that smells peculiar, could it possibly be marijuana? and Timothy, I must say, is no great help. There are a lot of men from the fire department here. I would much appreciate your aid in coping.''

As he came back in with her, she said, ''Well, did you and Mrs. Grahn have a nice chat?''—looking defiantly at the black-clad woman at the counter tearing romaine lettuce into pieces.

Her face was very pale, Marcia's, the blue eyes unnaturally and almost feverishly bright; they met his without wavering.

Not for the first time in his life, and half admiringly, he thought, You're as tough as an old iron hoop.

SIX

"Well, some say their prayers, and some meditate on the fleetin' quality of all life—and some steal spoons," a soft voice behind Tike said.

Tike had been shoveling the very old, soft silver apostle spoons from the drawer of the dining room buffet into her large cracked red leather handbag.

She turned with her three-cornered white grin to face Sophie.

Calmly, she said, "Last time I was here, he said, I want you to have those apostle spoons, Tike, seeing you like them so much. Eventually, you know, he meant."

"I never knew you were of an artistic bent much less pious, Matthew and Mark and Luke and company to stir your demi-tasse. But of course, they're worth a mint of money, he bought them at Sotheby's in London ten, eleven years ago. Suppose I said he said to me, Sophie, I want you to have a Monet, a Manet, and a Matisse, seein' you like them so much."

Tike gave her rippling giggle.

"You're a riot, Sophie."

"I must check Marcia to see if there's an inventory of the valuables in this house," Sophie said. "She's good at that kind of thing. Put those back, Tike."

"Make me," Tike said.

Sophie was standing very close to her, tall, supple; as tall as Tike, bigger, and in her soft way exuding a feeling of strength, of menace.

Tike, in whose view any kind of authority was to be either ignored or kicked in the shins, went on, "I get around, you know. I heard somewhere—I forget, someone at *Vogue*—that Sophie Converse, Inc., is in a pile of trouble. Money trouble. So of course you'd be worried about the spoons, now that I think about it. Here. Here's one for you, Sophie."

Sophie went very pale.

"Yes, our worlds touch," she said. "You hear things about me, I hear things about you. I was workin' with a photographer who shall be nameless, and he said, Overexposure—and believe it or not, he didn't mean your mammary glands, such as they are—that one's burnin' herself out. Fast."

She turned and walked away.

Vin, with an arm flung across his eyes, lay sleeping on one of the twin beds in the little yellow room over the garage, one of three small guest bedrooms Phip had put in, above the sparrows' nests.

Glenna was studying herself, hard, in the pier glass. Well-cut beige pants, beige cashmere sweater over an open-necked white shirt—

"Congratulations at looking so good in a sweater at the age of forty-five," Vin had said earlier, while they were dressing.

"It's tough, as I always say," Glenna answered obliquely, "to be the only ordinary flat-out housewife with all the brains and talent and style around."

Her hair was short, dark, in careless springing curls. Her skin was lightly freckled, looking scrubbed to a porcelain polish under a faint glow of makeup. Her eyes were hazel and thickly lashed.

In the mirror, she consciously put on the expression Vin liked. Good-natured, easygoing face when it was arranged, a flippant curve to the lips.

"What a relief you are after false eyelashes and boots."

"I'm not sure it's good to be that kind of relief."

There was a waking mutter from the bed. She went into the bathroom and took another tranquilizer.

Vin was propped up on one elbow when she went back into the room. His dark hair was tousled, the skin of his face, too robustly red, marked on one side with pillow creases.

"Well," he said, "business as usual at the same old stand. Well-known but aging advertising executive so broken up by his uncle's death that he overcompensates on gin and tumbles down the stairs."

She saw tears in his eyes. He turned his head away from her and continued, over his still strong and shapely bare shoulder, "It's a nice change, though, I could use a wake a week. Away from it all with an ironclad excuse. —A kid of twenty-six sending back a plan of mine on Havemeyer Petroleum to be rewritten. 'I'm sure you want to rethink this, Vin.' *Vin,* yet! . . . And after you rethink it, Vin, the men's room needs a good scrubbing. . . .' "

"Darling," Glenna said softly, "you seem to be forgetting what particular wake you're at."

His shoulders lifted in a long sigh. "Yes, for a minute I did forget that part of it. But the luck of the former, very former, rocketing young advertising star seems to be taking a turn for the worse. What if—whether or not someone sped him on the way to the cemetery, oh Christ, that sounds cruel—but what if he scrambled together some kind of crazy piece of paper and had it witnessed and hid it somewhere? What if *he* decided to rethink it? We're back where we were, up to our asses in the soup."

"You'd better watch yourself, Vin. They're all eager too, their tongues hanging out, I'm sure, but they're too smart to show it. Except, maybe, Marcia."

"What do you mean, Glenna, watch myself? Are you afraid that if they get pushed into a corner they'll tag me and hand me over to the police just to clear the air?" His tone was almost bantering. "I must say you're a great help if it ever did come down to the short strokes. Running off to old mither in Scarsdale Tuesday like someone out of afternoon television, just before the soap commercial. 'No, Officer, I can't vouch for my husband's whereabouts Tuesday night, we'd quarreled and I'd left the house—' "

Glenna went over to him and kissed him. "Shut up, Vin love, take a shower, and then I think your other suit, there's a little tear in the knee of the blue, those damned plank floors, but it can be rewoven—"

"All right. But I wish you wouldn't sound so sad."

"I suppose," Garrett Converse said to his brother Leo, "the will's all right?"

They were striding the moors in a mutual escape from the flowers, and the family, and their brother's body.

"I suppose it is," Leo said. "*I* haven't received any new instructions."

"I wish you could insert a bit more ringing confidence into your voice. This wild story of the housekeeper's—I wonder if there's any possibility that Phip got a bit . . . funny, toward the end?"

"I doubt that. I talked to him, oh, three weeks ago, about our annual review of his affairs. That was slated for next week. Which isn't to say that he might not have wanted to marry the female."

He added gloomily, "Men do, all kinds and ages and conditions of men." His own wife had died ten years ago; he had been very fond of her. "And, of course, Phip liked his drink, he thought up Hearth Homes after half a bottle or so, he might have gotten carried away. . . ."

Phip's will had never been made a secret. Equal shares of his estate to go to his brothers, his sister, and his nieces and nephews; the third generation left to reap its own benefits from its parents' holdings.

"How does it stand now?" Garrett asked. "About half a million apiece? Not counting the collection—"

"Art market's not what it might be. But even so. Yes, that's about right. Including the absentees, of course, Jack's mother, and Hugh."

The salt wind stirred Garrett's thick white hair. He lifted a hand that shook a little to smooth it back.

"The will—if *that's* what's been bothering you, I don't know that I'd worry about it," Leo said.

Kate was making for the stairs to snatch a brief nap, or at

least a rest, in the room to the right of the top of the stairs, the room she always slept in at Phip's, and for which she had a great affection.

At night the great lantern of Highland Light swept it solemnly, regularly, on the minute, every minute; disturbing until you got used to it and then soothing, like the eye of God flashing benevolently upon you, guarding your slumbers.

In the little hall she passed necessarily very close to Jack, who had just run down the stairs.

They stopped and exchanged gazes and, she thought, in a way refreshed themselves with each other for a moment.

"My firemen are very heavy going," Jack murmured. "You wouldn't want to come back with me and charm them?"

"No, it's a"—she covered a yawn—"long time since six-fifteen this morning. But, while we're here . . ."

"What, Kate? While we're here?"

"Is there something wrong with Garrett? He keeps watching you as though you were a grenade about to go off in his face."

"I don't want," Jack said slowly, "to tell tales out of school. But, Kate, take a guess or two. You're, for the moment, a member of the United States Senate, and I'm a member of the press. In Washington."

He studied her face with its faint glaze of fatigue. "Do guess, Kate. I'm beginning to feel somewhat alone in this crew and I want very badly—after you get up—to have someone to talk to."

Kate said, after perhaps thirty seconds, "Is he about to be under investigation, or indicted, for something illegal and immoral, if not fattening? Is the Washington *Post* going to drop on him? Or the *Times?* And is he watching you to see *if* you know, and *what* you know, and how soon it's going to happen?"

"I can see," he said, "I'll have at least one person on the same wavelength. Have a nice sleep. But a quick one. Don't, for God's sake, abandon me."

He was temporarily saved from his firemen by the priest's arrival. They retreated respectfully to the far end of the room when the stocky, richly rounded, black-suited figure appeared.

"Well, Bishop, greetin's," Sophie said.

"And the same to you, Mother Superior."

He beamed at Sophie, smiled at Marcia, but after a short spell on the kneeler zeroed in on a comforting male presence, you knew where you stood, with a man: Jack Converse. They had met once, over drinks, at Phip's.

"I don't know if you remember," he said. "Father McAloon. Kevin McAloon. I've met you—not in church, I think, I connect you in some way with the grog."

Jack remembered him very well. The priest had endeared himself forever to Phip by attempting to explain to his congregation, on Trinity Sunday, when Phip had paid one of his rare visits to mass, the nature of the Trinity. He had called upon them to summon up a mental picture of a brewer's well-known three-ring symbol, and to aid them further in comprehension had added amiably, in his pronounced Boston Irish accent, the brewery's slogan: "Purity, bawdy, and flavor."

He was a man in his late forties, with shining round pink cheeks and very large innocent gray eyes and a tonsure contributed not by the razor but by the disappearance of all but a half circle of very black hair.

Jack listened politely to kind platitudes about Phip, and death, and God's will. Having gotten through these, Father McAloon returned to being an individual: himself.

"Phip wasn't much for turning up for weekly mass . . . it's a small church and he said the people and all those walls gave him claustrophobia"— Father McAloon allowed himself a large wink and Jack was amused at his ambivalence: the naturally church-avoiding Irishman one and the same man as the shepherd with his flock—"but he was generous with his donations, very generous. In face . . . Is there somewhere we can go for a smoke? I don't like blowing it around Phip's head."

"Next room. A drink too, if you'd like."

"Outside, then, a drink later."

The firemen could now be heard in the dining room, busy with bottles.

The two men went out under the catalpa tree. Slanting sun glistened on Father McAloon's cheeks. He said abruptly, "It's not like it was in the old movies any more, is it? Where they'd all come home from the cemetery and sit in a circle in the library while the lawyer cleared his throat and read the will?"

"I'd hardly think so. Did he say he'd leave your church some little remembrance?"

"Not so little," Kevin McAloon said. "Ten thousand dollars."

He took out a large white handkerchief and nervously wiped his brow. "Or so he always *said*, you know. It's awkward, rattling silver like this at the edge of the grave, so to speak, but it's a small church, and poor, and somehow we have less and less people coming, and the bills are on me like a sack of potatoes on my back. . . ."

The opportunity was too good to miss.

Jack was not given to winking but there was a suggestion of it in his voice as he asked, "As Phip's priest and spiritual adviser, you'd be in his confidence. Did he ever say anything to you about marrying Mrs. Grahn? His housekeeper?"

The shining face and the eyes were not good at concealment. Jack thought he saw guilt, surprise, concern, embarrassment, and distaste—and fear?—each expression clearly and faithfully following the other, chase across Father McAloon's countenance.

He thought he might be wrong, but, reading the face, that the priest might not only have known but have been the one who informed someone in Phip's family about the impending marriage.

"Marrying? *Marrying*. No indeed," Father McAloon said, and blushed as violently as his already high coloring allowed.

The blush could be that of a bachelor shrinking at the idea of such a marriage; or an honest man's shame at telling an outright lie to another man's face.

But Jack felt he had already gotten an answer to his question. Not quite knowing what to do with the answer yet, where to put it, he said, "My Uncle Leo is Phip's lawyer. When he comes back, I'll have him call you about the bequest."

He had a sudden fantastic mental picture of the priest attempting to administer to Phip the last sacraments of the Church, a benign ear asking for Phip's unintended final confession, the tall white blessed candle lit on the bedside table, the wafer of the Host waiting to be slipped between the lips—and then, intent upon his ten thousand dollars for his starving church, and in a quick and strong and humane manner, murdering Phip. . . .

"And now will you have a drink, Father?"

"I will," Father McAloon said fervently. "I will indeed. And if I may say so, you look as if you could use a drop yourself."

SEVEN

As if she were playing a new sort of party game, Tike addressed the room gaily. "Where were we all on the night Uncle Phip died? In case that man Dutra comes back, and not just to pray and drink?"

She had changed out of her forties clothes into house painter's bib overalls made of heavy dull white satin, and a severely tailored shirt of smoky brown chiffon without, as her long, graceful movements often indicated, a bra.

She looked ravishing; and casually dangerous.

They had all moved as if by mutual consent away from the room with the coffin, into the big, long room behind it, Phip's library-bedroom.

It was a time of day they had more or less to themselves. The simple and homely had left for their five o'clock supper and television. The gleaming and important, valuing their own drink and dinner hours, would drop around later, or tomorrow, from Wellfleet and Boston and Long Island and Manhattan.

There was something to Marcia's cocktail-party accusations, Kate thought; this was the second one today. Everybody, as though party-bound, was in different clothing.

Jack had lit a fire. He looked thoughtfully around and then came and sat down by Kate on the big squashy brown velvet sofa. His side touched hers, lightly; there was a sense of muscles, vigorous, like a stirring of fish under smooth water.

He seemed to pour out a relishing aura of life, of immediacy, almost as visible as a cloud of smoke above and around his dark head. He made the very air she was breathing tingle.

Ignite the rockets. Strike up the band, Sophie had said.

Well, yes.

"As nobody seems anxious to say where they were and what they were up to, I'll begin," Tike said. "I was in bed with a professor of archaeology. Which makes him sound elderly, his job, I mean, but he's not, he's fun."

The telephone rang. It was Neiman-Marcus for Sophie. In black which, long and slender and seductive, had nothing to do with death, Sophie went to the telephone and made soft drawling sounds into it, concluding, "Of *course* not . . . it's a crock of the well-known article."

Coming back to her chair, she said, "As Tike has taken it upon herself to put a question to the assemblage, I'll speak for one and maybe all. My answer is, and I just heard it ten minutes ago, tomorrow will be fair and pleasant, with brisk winds fifteen to twenty miles an hour, average wave heights at Race Point six to ten feet, small-craft warnin's out."

Marcia, who had been looking horrified, about Tike's costume, and her question, and her archaeologist, said in a bright tired voice, "Always a lovely time of the year, here."

Nobody had any further observations to make, on the weather.

The telephone again. Timothy, closest to it, picked it up, listened, and said, covering the receiver, "*Could* there be anyone named Eugenia, any more? For you, Jack." A man of flesh and blood suddenly emerging from behind his bland bored look, "Nice voice, sexy."

"I'll take it next door," Jack said. "Tell her to hang on."

He was back in about four minutes. Kate wouldn't have given it a moment's thought twenty-four hours ago. Jack's girl, calling him. She gave it a moment's thought now.

It would be nice, sensible, if he'd sit somewhere else. He was not only back beside her, he leaned across her to reach for a table lighter to her left, the contact brief and, odd word to present itself to her, splendid.

"Now that we're alone," he said to his family, his voice seeming to vibrate over her skin, "I don't see anyone standing in line to hear Mrs. Grahn's tale."

"I assumed that if she'd handed you a bomb you would have dropped it by now," Leo growled. "Pack of hysterical nonsense. I suppose?"

"She hasn't anything in writing, about the marriage. And no proof of her accusations. Or nothing she can put a finger on yet. She's waiting for God to guide her."

"Leo." Marcia's voice was half imploring, half commanding. "That woman must be silenced."

"How would you propose to do that?" Leo asked. "Short of a gun, or a noose, or a pair of extremely efficient hands?" He fitted his own long, strong hands around his neck, thumbs centered under his Adam's apple.

"Can't you get rid of her, send her out of the house?"

"Can't you pay her off?"

"Threaten her with libel, prison—"

Three almost simultaneous suggestions, from Glenna, Tike, Marcia.

"Any or all of those moves would just bolster her position." Leo took a thirsty pull at his drink. "How do you think it would sound to, say, someone in Jack's profession? 'Instead of ignoring me, as innocent people would do, they threw me out of the house . . . tried to buy me off . . . threatened to jail me.' "

"I agree," Jack said. "Better to keep her here where we can watch her if her pot boils over, or her God shows up in the kitchen."

Timothy, who had been standing beside the baby grand piano at the opposite end of the room from the bed, covered for daytime in leopard-printed velvet and stacked with pillows, lifted the piano's lid idly and then bent forward with sudden interest. There was a label gummed under the lid.

"For my dear Jack, when, if ever, I depart this earth," he read. "Long may you play."

Kate turned her head in time to see the naked flicker of surprise, and love, and sorrow on Jack's face.

"Not bad," Timothy went on. "A Bechstein. Is it in tune, I wonder?"

He struck a few keys and then slowly, picking his way,

started to play the "Dead March" from *Saul*.

"Timothy, for God's sake," Garrett began from the deep chair near the bed where he had been silently sitting. Marcia's voice galloped over and above his.

". . . in a house of death—stop that, stop it immediately!" She got up nervously from the other end of the sofa. "I wonder if *everything* in the house is labeled? That dining room table, Queen Anne, 1738 or earlier, I believe, Phip told me the experts told him it's better than the one in the Metropolitan Museum—Leo, what's the position here?"

"Apart from a few special and particular gifts, like the piano—which by the way I didn't know about—Phip left his personal possessions to be divided up among us, amiably and willy-nilly." He smiled his sardonic deep-creased smile.

Tike, wanting center stage again, gave her father a head-to-foot look.

"Speaking of where everybody was," she said, grinning, "and like did someone hurry Uncle Phip on his way—maybe Daddy was dipping his fingers into the estate. And the annual review of all that money coming up. After all, it *is* a lawyer thing to do."

Vin had been very quiet: a quiet so determined, so noticeable, that it struck the ear as loud. He had come into the room showered and brushed and handsomely clothed in dark gray. His composure exploded.

"If you won't do it," he said to Leo, "I will."

He got up and walked over to Tike and struck her hard, across the cheek. She staggered.

Kate thought she heard Jack say softly, "Well played."

"Well, fuck you, you old *flop!*" Tike cried. "Toby Towers, he's going to be the next president at your place, right? Twenty-six, he's one of my things, and the killing part of it is that I met him at your house, you were scared not to invite him to the party, I guess—you should hear what he thinks about you. He calls you the Antique Shop . . . like, guess what the Antique Shop said yesterday, in a meeting. . . . You don't even make his shit list, you're like on your way out at any minute now—"

Without in any way hurrying, Leo took four long strides, picked up his daughter effortlessly in his arms, and above her furious screaming said, "Jack, lock the back door, I'll take care of the front. I believe the windows are well secured."

He carried her, her white satin legs kicking, feet bare, out of the room and out the front door and in a moment came back in to the sound of a heavy strap latch falling into place.

"Let her," he said, his voice calm but his cheeks patched with raw red, "address her obscenities to the catalpa tree."

Sophie's eye caught Kate's. "Like, to borrow yet another four-letter word from the family trash heap, I predicted, on the plane. Remember?"

She got up and went to Vin and put her arms around him and kissed him. "Whatever you've got in that shop of yours, Vin darlin', I'm buying," she said. Kate wondered if some kind of realignment was taking place; possibly against Sophie's First Prize.

She found herself staring at the silver-framed photographs, oval and oblong and round, on the shelf of the fine large mahogany writing desk facing her.

Marcia and her husband, Daniel, leaning on the rail of an ocean liner, a picture from long, long ago, both of them young and gay. Marcia not pretty, but with a delicate crisp distinction of feature.

Vin and Glenna and Jack, wind-blown and sun-darkened, on Jack's sailboat, Vin personable and mirthful, saluting the camera with a crystal mug of beer that caught the light, a Jack not yet twenty laughing, too, at something, head thrown back. Glenna looking touchingly young and slender, as though her bones hadn't quite hardened yet.

A picture of herself, at about four, in a starched and smocked dress, sitting on a stone whippet, one of a pair crouched at the top of the steps climbing to the front door of Phip's town house; legs sticking out, plump, in white socks and Mary Janes. Face intent and solemn, hair cut in bangs.

Sitting side by side in the sunlight on the one single front step of the Truro house, her own adoptive—how she disliked the word, she loved them in a comfortable daughterly way—her adoptive parents, Hugh and Livia Converse. Hugh only slightly less tall than Leo, but with gaiety around his wide slender-lipped mouth. Livia ridiculously young and charming, something gangly about her long legs, although she must have been forty when the picture had been taken. A sense of closeness, of love for each other, coming from the black and white oblong like a whiff of warmth from the fire. From Hong Kong, they had cabled flowers; Hugh couldn't get away.

Sophie in a hammock, lying lazily on her side; Sophie at perhaps twenty-nine, the year she was married. (I wonder, Kate thought, as a shoulder, a speaking shoulder, moved restlessly against hers, is twenty-nine a good age to marry at?) Sophie had been through a rough divorce three years ago and was in her own words in no hurry to dive back into the shark pond again.

Leo and his dead wife, Grace, dressed for tennis, curiously alike, she very tall too, with an atttractive three-cornered face and Timothy's sparkling dark eyes.

Reading the *Times* under the catalpa tree, Garrett, looking up over the top of his paper, fresh-faced and untroubled, alight with power, with success.

The framed faces, cherished by Phip, seemed so very far away from these people, this room. She felt for some reason open to every hurt, every surge of emotion, the dartings of jealousy, avarice, secrecy, and love and fear, moving among the firelit shadows.

Jack: "He's never had anyone of his own, just relatives to borrow. . . . If someone near and dear came at you in the dark . . ."

Breathing was suddenly difficult. She started convulsively to rise and he turned his head and said, his voice very low and startling her, "If you must run away, don't be long."

"Want some air that doesn't reek with Converse?" Sophie asked sympathetically. "You're lookin' a bit fragile, can't say I blame you . . . but don't let Tike back in."

She went out by the back door and around the house. She saw a glimmer of white in the light from the front windows, Tike, sitting on the grass leaning against the bole of the catalpa tree, arms hugging her knees. Going around the far end of the hedge so as not to have to pass close to her, she called unwillingly, "Are you cold, Tike?"

"Not as cold as someone else is going to be," Tike said

sullenly. An empty threat from a tearing-down sort of girl, put out of the house by her father, like a cat or dog? Or perhaps something real in her hand, some weapon.

She climbed the long slope to the moors and gratefully gulped the air, smelling of the sea, and long grass that had blown in the sun all day, and bayberry and sweet fern.

Her abrupt and necessary flight caused her to miss, by just a few minutes, the visit of Mr. Thomas Spiggott.

EIGHT

Timothy answered the door when the knocker sounded, a light apologetic bang.

When he opened it, Mr. Spiggott looked with some apprehension at the silky black hair touching his eyebrows, and the glittering examining eyes. Really, were there no . . . reliably ordinary people here?

There was the girl behind him, sitting under the tree, who when he had almost fallen over her and said, "Er—hello there," hadn't troubled to answer him. But he did remember seeing a gray-haired woman in an efficient felt hat. . . .

"Spiggott," he said to Timothy.

Timothy was openly puzzled. "Faucet?—A drink of water? The kitchen is—"

"No, no, Spiggott, Thomas Spiggott, I wonder if I might briefly pay my respects to—"

"Oh yes, sorry, in here."

Mr. Spiggott, of Presbyterian persuasion, would have no part of the kneeler, but stood quietly by the coffin, looking down at Phip. Timothy waited at a polite distance, thinking he should offer him a drink, after he finished meditating, or praying, or just gazing, or whatever he was doing.

Not that he looked like a man with any particular fancy for the bottle; small and lean, his scholarly head a little too large for his body; thin untidy gray hair, heavy eyeglasses, a dusty look to his gray flannel trousers and well-worn heather tweed jacket.

The door into the back room was open. There was a low buzz of conversation, a ringing of the phone, a voice saying, "For you, Garrett, Washington, where else?"

Timothy had been right. Mr. Spiggott politely declined a drink. After another doubtful look at his young host pro tem, he went to the doorway of the room beyond and stood hesitantly in it.

From behind, Timothy announced, "Mr. Thomas Spiggott come to see Uncle Phip—"

Mr. Spiggott raised a hand in horror at invading, intruding, having to be introduced to the entire, daunting roomful of people.

"I don't want to disturb the family in any way. . . ." His eye lit on Leo, awkwardly tall even in a sitting position, on a loveseat beside the gray-haired woman, now dressed in long dark brown silk.

"It's just that—is there someone—ah—I might have a few words with? In private. As I say, I don't want to disturb you, any of you—"

That towering man, with his expression of being prepared for the worst, would be the one to talk to.

Suddenly aware of a glance almost burning its way into his left side, he turned and saw the blue gaze, brilliantly intent, of the young man on the brown velvet sofa. Nothing whatever of resignation or gloom about him, but an embracing of here and now, an interest and curiosity so marked that Mr. Spiggott almost thought he heard the words, "Who really are you and what is it you have to tell?" This, although the man on the sofa hadn't opened his mouth.

He looks, Mr. Spiggott thought, momentarily wandering off the point he was going to have to make, as though he'd be interested to hear about the holly fern, the only one he had ever seen, on this part of the Cape. He looked as if he was interested, with all of himself, in everything.

Perhaps, he thought—Leo coming toward him, introducing himself, "Leo Converse. Just through the living room, there, into my brother's office"—perhaps after all he'd gotten the wrong man to talk to.

Phip's office was pleasantly unbusinesslike with its blue floor and ruffled organdy curtains and deep chairs and walnut slant-front desk, old, valuable, many-drawered. Over a small metal filing cabinet, on which had been placed a white pitcher of bayberry and nun's money, hung an attractive large watercolor, blurred, blue and white, breathing windy speed and almost sounding of gurgling water, sailboats racing.

Leo thought, and hoped, that he was one of the few people who knew that when the watercolor was reversed, the Degas proclaimed itself, "Woman Braiding Her Hair," the frame flush with the canvas so as to create a completely flat surface. Phip, annoyed with insurance regulations, disobediently allowed himself the company of his treasures, here and there.

Thinking of the Bechstein, Leo made a mental note to secure the Degas. God knew who would take a fancy to the watercolor.

"Now then, Mr. Spiggott," he said. "What can I do for you?"

Jack had gotten up from the sofa a minute or two after they left the room and, without offering explanations—people do in the normal way occasionally leave sofas and drinks, however comfortable—went out the back door of the kitchen.

He nodded at Mrs. Grahn, who was stirring something in a pot on the black iron stove; and then went around and stood against the wall of the house, close to one of Phip's office windows. Because of the mild night, and the smoke, and the pouring sweetness of the flowers, the screened lower half of the window was open.

He had looked, first, out of the dining room window. Tike was nowhere to be seen.

Mr. Spiggott, sitting on a Hitchcock chair, explained that he was a retired certified public accountant, and that his avocation was identifying and collating the flora of the Cape, and—with a faint blush—that he had modest hopes he might someday find a publisher—

"Yes, yes," Leo said with Converse impatience. "Yes, an

interesting study. What was it that . . . ?''

Mr. Spiggott's story, with a few side trips into particularly
fascinating specimens snipped short by Leo, was that he had
had Phip's permission to investigate and tag and sketch the
plants in the old herb garden at the back of the house.

He was a poor sleeper and, planning a whole section on
night-scented varieties, often put his sleeplessness to good use.
A long browsing walk took him past the Converse house and,
on sudden impulse, he turned in at the opening in the privet
hedge and went around to the herb garden.

He hadn't wanted to use his flashlight, as it might startle or
disturb Mr. Converse, put him in mind of prowlers; but he did
employ, to excellent advantage, his nose, as he moved delicately on hands and knees along the edge of the garden, sniffing
out like a detective lovage and samphire, pennyroyal, rue,
borage, summer savory, ''and the very rare mothroot, a most
exciting discovery. . . .''

He was close to the window when he heard Mr. Converse
saying, or rather crying out, "No, oh *no* . . . ,'' the final *no*
slipping off into a blur. A plane had gone over just then, Mr.
Spiggott supposed from its comparatively low altitude a jet
heading for Logan in Boston. After the engine sounds died
away, there was absolute silence. There were no lights in the
bedroom and the curtains were drawn.

He had remained in a kneeling position, paralyzed, terrified.

"The voice—I can't tell you, I can't describe it—like coming
up from the bottom of a well—"

A dark chill overtook the listener outside the window.

After a time to get his knees back, Mr. Spiggott said, he
forced himself to his feet and went around to the front of the
house and knocked at the door. He was answered with profound
quiet. He knocked again, and waited for six minutes by his
watch, and then told himself he was an interfering old fool,
and turned and walked slowly out onto the road, and to the
crossroads where he had parked his car, and home.

Guiltily, he said, "I thought on deliberation that he might
have been having a bad dream, a man's dreams are his own
business. Or that he was talking to someone on the telephone
and was responding to some kind of bad news. I didn't want

to make a nuisance of myself, especially because it was with his permission that I could enter his private grounds at any hour. . . ."

Jack heard from Leo a prodding, throat-clearing sound.

". . . and, of course, very little crime out here, it's not like Provincetown. But there was, oh, six months ago, that poor old woman strangled in her house on Pamet Road, nobody ever found the culprit. . . ."

"Deplorable," Leo said in a tone of strained patience. "But I don't quite see—"

"And then," in a last attempt to Leo to clear his conscience, transfer his burden, "it could have been a cry of sudden pain— his heart—"

Leo, having scoured Mr. Spiggott's decks of his information and questions and conclusions, took over.

Authoritative voice from his special cavern, reverberating: "Let's sum up this visit. What is it that you're suggesting? If anything?"

"I feel I . . ." The other man's voice faltered. "Perhaps I should have called a doctor, or the police, instead of just turning my back and walking away as people do these days. I feel I should have been more forceful—resuscitation might have been applied. . . . The truth is I was badly frightened. . . . Was . . . was everything in order?"

"Yes. Sad as it may be, my brother died an expected *and* orderly death. My advice to you is not to dwell on your morbid fancies, man. That way madness lies. The best and most appropriate thing you can now do, for yourself and for my brother and for his family, is to dismiss this whole matter."

He took out his handkerchief and made a trumpeting noise that could be interpreted as grief.

"And now will you have a drink?"

"I think"—the voice deflated, embarrassed—"perhaps a touch of brandy. . . ."

On Mr. Spiggott's departure, Leo returned to his family. His entrance caused a peculiar simultaneous dying down of voices.

Vin spoke for the rest of them. "A few words in private—did he have anything to add to the story of the alleged romance?"

There was a sense of breaths being held.

"No," Leo rumbled. "He'd borrowed fifty-five dollars from Phip last week and wanted to return it to the estate."

"Really," Timothy said rather than asked. "What a very conscientious man he must be."

"I suppose," his father said, "it would appear odd to you, yes."

"I do hope he hadn't—in addition—anything unpleasant to say," Marcia said. As the family Memory, she added, "Whenever you're not telling the exact truth, Leo, you squint a little with your left eye, you always did and I suppose you always will."

Jack left his post and went slowly, hands in his pockets, head bent, through the aspen trees and up the slope to the moors.

An orderly death, Mr. Spiggott. Yes.

". . . the bedclothes all roiled and thrashed around, I tidied them to make the bed more comfortable. . . ."

Death throes.

Odd that you could live in, work in, a world beating with pain and terror, corruption and disaster, torture and treachery and slaughter, and find it almost impossible to believe that one man, in your own family, had met with any kind of fatal mishap, had been, slip quickly over the word, killed.

At the hands of someone of your own blood, or someone connected with your blood.

Mr. Spiggott at the front door, for six minutes. If the impossible was true, someone might, someone would, have heard his knock and be waiting, too, watching, listening over the pounding of a trapped and terrified heart—

He tried to remember about the outside front light. It was usually switched off when Phip went to bed, he was subject to minor thrifts. The man outside the door, if seen by vague starlight, would probably have been taken as a late caller, or so the listener inside would hope.

It had obviously not occurred to Mr. Spiggott, walking into a possible lion's den, that while he saw nobody, he might have been seen by somebody.

Not that his information amounted to anything concrete. Another whiff of cold mist.

Jack himself had seen and heard men die; the sounds were never attractive and were by the wise and sane dismissed as soon as possible from the mind.

That way, Mr. Spiggott, madness lies.

He wondered if Phip's housekeeper was given to standing, with attentive ears, at interesting closed doors.

Back there in her kitchen, Mrs. Grahn, busy with her creamed potatoes, Mrs. Grahn. Waiting for her God to suggest to her what if anything to do with her accusations.

It would be instructive to know which particular God she worshiped, a God of vengeance, or one of love and forgiveness and peace, or one of righteousness at all costs.

At all costs. . . . It was too late, Phip was dead, and she couldn't prove anything, she had only her convictions and her claimed expert knowledge on the state of Phip's health from hour to hour to go on. Nothing she had to say could set the machinery of the law in motion, stop the wake, stop the funeral, fill in an order for the autopsy.

And Phip was Mr. Philip Andrew Converse, valued resident of the town, patron of the little church, mourned by a police chief, and the fire department; and a rich man, a very rich man.

While she was just Stella Grahn, housekeeper.

But if her Deity's advice was, Damn the torpedoes, full speed ahead, there could be hell to pay.

He found himself disturbed by his own reactions.

Was he prepared to blink an eye, look the other way, if he really thought Phip had been killed?

Cover it up, along with the rest of the family, bury the matter six feet underground?

He was not now, at his age, particularly concerned about money, about security. He made a reasonable salary and liked very much his life, his work. He was able honestly to rid himself of any mentally obstructing concern about his own share of Phip's fortune being tied up, locked away. This was not what was causing the ambivalence.

But—leave out the rest, and their known or unknown financial needs—there was Marcia, completely dependent on Phip's money. And Vin, with dragons lashing their tails close on his heels.

Vin had been kind to him, when he was so very much the younger; treated him gracefully, as an intelligent adult; taught him his own lightning cutthroat tennis; seen him safely to bed at weddings, when he was learning how to drink but hadn't yet grasped the traps champagne could lay for a very young man.

Sophie, amiable worldly Sophie—"not that I believe that woman's romantic ramblin's. . . ."

He knew in a way too much but not enough about medicine. Misdiagnoses, malpractice suits, disastrous overlookings, suave cover-ups. After the thunderstorm and the scandal echoing and reechoing through the newspapers—

(Marvelous juicy story, objectively speaking, some reasonably well known names, photogenic faces, pretty women, politics in the person of a handsome senator, money, murder, the Converse collection. Colorful lives invaded, exposed. "Ms. Katherine Converse told police she spent the night of her uncle's death with a man named Ferdinand da Gama"?—So delightfully different from dull brutal daily killings.)

And with all that, the horror of committing pink serene dead Phip to the knife, the autopsy, the findings proving inconclusive or on the other hand completely satisfactory as far as apprehended physical evidence went.

Even though . . .

The gulfs, the arguments, doctor against doctor, with so much at stake.

He saw no choice now but to wait, wait perhaps a little dangerously, and see.

NINE

Kate sat near the edge of the cliff top a hundred yards up from Highland Light, her mind gratefully emptied, or almost.

The Atlantic crashed softly and peacefully far below. There was a bright moon dimmed now and then by fast-flying low emblazoned cloud. Sweet smells rose from the grasses around her.

Not really a peaceful coast, though. Phip had told her it was known, this lee of the Cape, as the graveyard of the Atlantic, and shown her a chart with a flock of innocent dots marking the sunken wrecks of ships caught by wind and waves and murderous currents and beaten to death.

"This disastrous shore," Thoreau had called it.

It didn't do, thinking about Phip's sunny house, or his quiet coffin within it, as neighboring on any disastrous shore.

She found herself musing about Vin, and Garrett. It was alarming to see what you had taken for years as family power, force, success, shaken at its base; a kind of permanency snatched away.

And Sophie—what was the private trouble that seemed to surface occasionally from under the lazy bantering manner?

Jack Converse kept interrupting the browsing of her mind like an exclamation point.

From nowhere a memory appeared, a Christmas when she was twelve. Leo's family had come to Hugh and Livia's Connecticut house and brought Jack and his mother with them.

There had been a holiday pack of children. They had built a great powdery white fort on the lawn and were having an amiable snowfight when Timothy, her own age, whacked her brutally in the head with a snowball that felt like a fist. "Dirty, *lousy*," she had heard, through a mist of pain, her cousin Jack say as he picked her up. "He put an old frozen apple into it . . ." and then he went over to the other side of the fort and knocked Timothy down.

There was a near rustle of footsteps in the grass. She turned and saw him, walking fast, the moonlight paling his blue shirt and silvering his long-legged fawn corduroys.

He sat down close beside her on the grass.

"Hello, Kate."

"Hello, Jack."

A light wind sprang up, coming off the sea, and she shivered a little.

"You're cold. . . ."

"No, the ground is warm." She didn't really know him well enough these days to be silent with him. "Where did you get those clothes? I didn't see you carrying a suitcase."

"I keep some here. In the room I usually sleep in, Marcia's in it now."

"You saw much more of Phip than anyone else, which makes me feel even guiltier—"

"I saw a lot but not enough, for what I owed him." He added without embarrassment or hesitation, "And I loved him."

Another silence; break it.

"You said you wanted to talk to me about things. . . ."

"Yes. This matter, first."

He put a strong arm around her and bent his head to her. He kissed her, lightly and exploringly, his lips firm and yet delicate, and said against the skin of her cheek, "How is it we don't know each other better?"

Confused, shaken, not knowing what to think—she had no idea of the ways he might amuse himself, with women, no compass points to go by, and he and Sophie were always, with each other, affectionate kissers—she pulled a little away from him.

He answered his own question, almost absent-mindedly.

"But then Hugh and Livia took you off to California when you were, what? fifteen. And when you came to New York, twenty-one, I was off to France with INS. And when we met again, I think you were twenty-three or so, I was in love with a girl. You went to England to work for a year in Mall and Mall's London office and before you came back I went to Washington. . . ."

She had the strangest feeling he was in two places; here with her and very far away.

"You keep fading and coming in again like a radio wave from Tokyo or somewhere . . . , well, weddings and funerals, as you said. And parties."

"Yes, you with your companion and I with mine, ships passing. Astonishing, when you think about it." His hand closed on her forearm. "Yes, you are cold. Don't be coy, Kate, come back here to me."

"I'm *not* coy," she said half angrily. "It's just that I don't—"

He moved her head into a delicious position between his chin and his shoulder, and with his fingertips examined the shape of her eyebrows, the rounding of a temple, the slope of one cheek, and then a small earlobe with a hoop of tiny pearls dangling from it.

How warm he was. And the vitality you felt when he entered a room was, this close, unnerving, piercing.

Yes, her cousin Jack, affectionate, loving, wanting to know her better.

If it were any other man, or relationship, she would know without question she was beginning to be made love to. But how horribly embarrassing it would be to step off the tightrope of family, and have him say, bewildered, Kate, for God's sake, we met when you were two and I was five, what's all the maidenly fuss about?

She found a word, an explanation, that satisfied her for the moment, clarified things, and made them, or should make them, easy and natural.

Comfort.

He wanted it from her; he wanted to give it to her.

Death, annihilation—even unshadowed, straightforward death—terrified people, drew them together, reminded them that merely to be alive was a fine and happy, a priceless state. Or at least for a little while, until mental and emotional balances were adjusted, and the specter, the inevitability, was firmly stored away in the dark.

It was not, she thought, a moment to be stingy and self-conscious.

She hugged him back heartily and said, "That was nice of Phip, the piano."

She felt his chin lift from the top of her head. He laughed a little, softly.

"And," he said, "as Sophie reported, average wave heights at Race Point six to ten feet, small-craft warnings out—changing the subject with a crash. Well, we can return to it, Kate. Later."

What subject?

"About my sounding like a fading radio wave from Tokyo . . . something happened a little while back. I shouldn't dump it on you but I will, because I don't know what the hell to make of it."

He told her about Mr. Spiggott.

The moon came out from behind a cloud and showed him an unreal blued face, the eyes very large.

"It's hard," she said after a silence, "to be analytical, or even intelligent, about such a horrible—your mind backs away from it."

"Yes. You grab at the other explanations. All perfectly possible. —What am I saying, I mean likely." He added as if to himself, "If I know Leo, he's kept the interview to himself. I hope so, anyway."

She moved restlessly and said, "I suppose we ought to be getting back, I've had my sabbatical, in fact I shouldn't have left at all but I thought the walls were going to fall down on me."

"I know." He got to his feet with an effortless springing motion and reached his hand to her and drew her up.

"No, don't try to take your hand away. I want it. Besides, you need guidance, you might just twist an ankle in a rabbit hole, or walk into a clump of bayberry and brambles and get all scratched."

Hand in hand, they walked back over the clean windy scented moors to Phip's house.

As they were descending the slope to the aspen trees, a car that looked, in the diffused light from the front windows, to be a vintage MG, a shining dark color, possibly green, drew up at the edge of the road under the tree.

"Well, finally," Tike said, her voice floating high and clear on the night air. *"Finally."* The slam of a door, and then the car shot down the road with deliberate unmufflered noisiness.

"Her pilot, maybe, temporarily grounded. I think that's her car," Jack said to Kate. "Brute, isn't she, Tike."

"You don't suppose Mrs. Groin has put somethin' sinister in these creamed potatoes?" Sophie said. "They taste odd. Good, though." She took a forkful.

"Or maybe it's in the curried shrimp, hot as goddamnit, you'd never notice it on your palate until it was too late—someone havin' to pick up the phone and call that obligin' undertaker boy with the nice gray gloves."

As there was no room on the buffet, with its ranks of bottles, Mrs. Grahn had placed a heatproof pad on the Queen Anne duck-footed table that had so concerned Marcia, covered it in heavy glossy white damask, and set out a splendid assortment of hot and cold dishes, two kinds of salad, her thin-crusted faintly sour Portuguese bread, hot, and a large cake with French chocolate icing, a bowl of fruit, and a board of cheeses.

No one being disposed to take his or her plate into the living room, there was something of a crush around the table, and in Phip's office across the hall.

Standing, eating with his fingers a leg of fried chicken, Timothy looked at the wall above the pitcher of bayberry and nun's money. "What happened to the watercolor?" he asked. "I could have sworn—"

Leo sat at Phip's desk morosely consuming a large portion of smoking steak and kidney pie, from which he occasionally turned his attention to his artichoke vinaigrette.

"Removed," he said to his son. "I wouldn't think it was your kind of thing, anyway, did you have a fancy for it?"

"Yes," Timothy said. "I remember it from when I was a

kid, I used to wonder how it could look so wet when it was dry, I kept going up to touch it to make sure.''

Leo registered a slight surprise; unlike Timothy to communicate, any longer, reveal even such a small scrap of himself.

There never had been any colossal battling. Timothy had dropped out of Yale after six months there and gently cut himself adrift from the New York brownstone, the sprawling cottage in East Hampton, his mother's charities, his father's clubs.

"Expect nothing from me if you're prepared to spit on our kind of life," Leo said.

"Naturally, I'll take care of myself until Uncle Phip's . . . fellowship comes through.''

Death possibly loosening his tongue now. Or maybe he knew what was on the back of the watercolor.

"Sophie told me, naming no names, someone was helping himself to valuables,'' Leo said, and added with genuine gloom, "I suppose we'll have to have some kind of informal meeting, dividing things up in a civilized fashion. I don't look forward to it.''

Mrs. Grahn came through, on her way from the kitchen to the dining room, with a fresh pot of coffee. She had changed back into her shirtwaist dress and sensible shoes. The marks of weeping had left her face; it was its usual iridescent white. Her curly hair glistened red-gold in the lamplight. She was impassive; a woman doing her duty by her late employer's family.

Which, Kate thought, was a little frightening. Looking at her, you would never know this efficient automaton had hurled her personal bomb into a roomful of people.

Was she sorry she had made a scene, and was she now making amends? Or merely keeping her hands busy, her shield up, doing what she was still being paid to do, while she considered her next move?

To many men, Kate also thought, she would be a temptingly pillowy kind of woman.

Glenna, beside her, hungrily eating chocolate cake — "I suppose a death in the family is grounds for throwing your diet to the winds for a day or so"—had been narrowly observing Mrs. Grahn.

"That woman," she murmured after the housekeeper had left the room, "is scary. I'm glad there's a lock on our bedroom door—where does she sleep, anyway, with the house and the garage bursting with people?"

Kate had no idea; she supposed that, with the family descending, Mrs. Grahn had moved herself and her belongings from whatever room she occupied and was staying now in North Truro or Provincetown.

"Although"—Glenna hesitated and then took another small slice of cake—"it could be the other way around. If her mad tale were true, which is nonsense. She may be worrying about the lock on *her* door; in case somebody felt like strangling her. . . ."

From behind Glenna, Jack signaled to Kate: a slight lifting of one eyebrow, and just the faintest sideways tilt of his head and shifting of his glance in the same direction.

Kate picked up her coffee cup and followed him into the room at the back of the house. His fire had burned low. He gave it a proprietary glance and placed another log on it.

"Kate . . ." He came back to where she stood, sipping coffee. "I know you're of voting age and no doubt blindingly bright at what you do, and you outclass me a bit in salary, but I want especially to ask you—don't laugh—not to fall into speculations about death and disaster with anyone, this evening."

His meaning was explicit. Someone in this family, Kate, could be very, very dangerous.

She looked up at him, unintentionally bathed her gaze in his, and then, finding it a little uncomfortable, looked over his shoulder at the shelf of photographs.

"All right. I'm off to bed soon in any case."

The small silver-framed one of her astride the stone whippet was gone. For a moment she felt dismissed from the Converse family, as when she had read the *Times* obituary.

"I'm going to go out for a while." He didn't say where or why and she gathered she was not invited.

". . . And I'm more or less talked out," she went on, "but I do sort of wonder what happened to my photograph."

"Is nothing sacred?" Jack said, following her glance at the shelf. "I suppose some light-fingered person—" and he smiled and took her coffee cup from her hand.

Whatever he was going to say or do next was forestalled by a thin throat-clearing noise.

Garrett emerged from the other side of the black and gold Coromandel screen that partially divided the reading and sleeping halves of the room.

"Bless us," he said. "Death and disaster, cloak and dagger, cops and robbers. My dear *Jack*."

He looked very large, tall, rosy, and confident; but Kate imagined the confidence was contributed by drink, and good food, and his family surrounding him in this safe little island of death in the salty night. Underneath the benign colorings his bones showed much more sharply than she remembered them, and there was still the haunted look at the back of his eyes.

Jack did not humble easily. He gave his uncle back a sparkling, jousting stare.

"It's too much Washington, maybe," he said. "But we're nowhere near Capitol Hill, are we? I must remind myself of that."

"There are other things you might remind yourself of," Garrett said with sudden cold fury. "Like decency, and honor. And concern for the name you bear. Which you happen to share with some other people."

"And let sleeping uncles rest," Jack said softly. "No matter what?"

"I hope," Garrett, leaving the room, said bitterly over his shoulder, "your story will be worth it, to you."

TEN

Your story.

Turning right, at the main crossroads in North Truro, in the black Ford he had rented at the airport, he thought about it.

Perhaps his ingrained habit of questioning, probing, looking under surfaces and behind visible images to see what was really there, was leading him astray.

But he'd felt that this one errand was an obvious necessity, and he might as well get on with it. And then, if everything was in order with Phip's doctor, close ranks with the rest of the family.

Let sleeping Phip lie.

The hill on the road leading to Provincetown mounted steeply from the crossroads. The speed limit was thirty-five miles an hour; not a wide road, curves, hills, and even this late in the season the possibility of ambling pedestrians, bicyclists, children, cats and dogs.

He had almost topped the hill when he saw in the driving mirror the glare of headlights uncomfortably close behind him. A black Cadillac, Vin's; before he took his eyes from the mirror he saw the vague shadowy pink and white of the other man, in the front seat beside Vin. Garrett.

Vin was by nature a tailgater. Jack remembered it from earliest childhood. "For God's sake pick up your feet," Vin would cry. "What do you think this is, a funeral cortege?"

His headlights showed a stretch of road clear and empty before him. He increased his speed to forty. The following

73

headlights stayed where they were, perhaps four feet behind him.

Just before he got to the narrow little neck of land where Pilgrim Lake would appear on his right, the bay on his left, he remembered a lane that climbed into the dunes. If the other car was heading for Provincetown, it would be nice to lose it with a little detour up the lane.

He swung right, and with a sporting screech the Cadillac swung right, too.

Oh well, some kind of game, restless men snatched out of their busy daily lives, a little grieving, a little bored, wanting to amuse themselves, playing follow my leader. Or staging a mock cavalry charge on wheels.

It was ridiculous, the cold sweat, the feeling that he was being hunted down like an animal.

But there was only one way, from here, to get to Provincetown, the road between the lake and the bay. All right, he thought, trying for calm, I'll play your little automobile game with you. Cars are grown-up toys, for a lot of people.

As well as being a traditional American way of releasing rage and frustration. *Let me at that wheel, man.*

He turned suddenly right again, into someone's driveway. Vin's front fender just missed the rear of the Ford. The Cadillac went on up the lane and then stopped. Jack reversed out of the driveway and drove too fast for comfort and safety—but there were no speed limits here—back to the road, the Cadillac now no more than two feet behind him.

He could only hope and assume that Vin didn't want to injure or kill himself and Garrett. Keeping to the speed limit, he drove on, past the lake on one side, the bay on the other, showing between motels a great shudder of diamonds in the moonlight; Vin's headlights, in their reckless embrace of the rear of the car, glaring white in the Ford's reptile-green vinyl interior.

Entering Provincetown, he took the left at the split in the road, Commercial Street. People, thank God, traffic to slow him, to slow Vin, houses, lights, bustle. The fish-processing factory looming against the night sky. A smell of blown-out grease from a restaurant fan was strangely reassuring, an ugly everyday smell.

He parked the Ford with an easy, assumed nonchalance across

the street from the restaurant where if necessary he would face them, get rid of them: the Flagship. Vin parked behind him.

Their car doors slammed almost simultaneously, three of them.

Jack walked back to the other car and over a deep anger said coolly, "I couldn't figure out whether it was you or me you wanted to kill, Vin. With the senator thrown in for good measure. Is this what, in the advertising business, you call riding herd? A taste of what I can expect if I don't shut up?"

Garrett said lazily, "Just wondering if you felt the need to get to a phone without an extension, but," laughing, "you'd be too easy a target in a lighted telephone booth."

"For God's sake," Vin asked, jovial, "can't you take a joke?"

Which joke? The dangerous hounding car, or being too easy a target, or what?

He said, crossing the street with them to the lighted forecourt of the Flagship, still gay with late flowers, "I'm indebted to you for one thing. It never occurred to me there might be collusion—not just one person to think about—in case there was dirty work not very far from the crossroads. Will you join me in a drink? To celebrate," he added, "our mutual survival, no thanks to either of you for that."

After he opened the heavy door, he felt the familiar creaking of the planked floors, heralding them. No wonder, he thought. Approximately six hundred pounds of Converses, coming in.

A large warm untidy fire burned in the huge fireplace as they turned to the bar, which was mounted on a massive dory, not looking touristy but as though it had been there forever.

"Jack, doll," the pleasant middle-aged barmaid said. "And what'll it be?"

He wanted ale; Vin, scotch, and Garrett, a brandy.

She waved aside Jack's billfold.

"On the house. When I think of the thousands he spent here . . ."

The restaurant was very nearly filled. At varnished wobbly-footed unmatched tables, lit with candles in wax-drooling bottles, people looked at the three tall striking men at the bar.

Not five feet away from him, Jack heard a woman say to the man across from her, "I don't know who they are, but I know they're *somebody*—"

"That's Senator Converse, you ass," the man hissed back.

"And one for you, Min," Jack said, as she leaned on her elbows on the bar, in front of them.

"Thanks, love, a small gin." She poured it and lifted her glass. "To Mr. C., God love him. I'll remember him in my prayers. If I had my way they'd follow his coffin to the cemetery with the Boy Scouts, the Girl Scouts, all four fire engines, the high school band, and the entire staff of this restaurant. Including the—"

From the piano in the center of the room, two attractive girls launched into "The Minstrel Boy."

"—including the piano players," Min said, and burst into tears.

The girls played it properly. Not a sentimental ballad to be wept to, over one too many beers; but hard, fast, strong and strumming, a summons to battle, a war song about death and loss and woe.

One of the girls started singing sweetly:

> "The Minstrel Boy to the war is gone,
> In the ranks of death you'll find him."

Min, sniffling, set fresh drinks in front of them. Vin's hand, lifting his scotch, shook. He watched while Jack poured his ale steadily.

> "One sword, at least, thy rights shall guard,
> One faithful harp shall praise thee. . . ."

Garrett raised his glass and said, "To Jack, Phip's one sword, one faithful harp, and all that crap." He sounded almost merry and amiable.

Min signaled Jack down a few steps, leaned over, and whispered, "I think what they're saying is dirty gossip, I don't believe a word of it."

He didn't dare ask, now, exactly what the dirty gossip was. Intended marriage, murder, or the two combined. "You're absolutely right," he whispered back, and went to finish his ale.

Knowing that the girls were playing the song for Phip, he

told Min to ask them what they would like to drink, emptied his glass with dispatch, and looked at his watch.

"I must leave you," he said. "Sorry."

"Nonsense, the night's young, we'll come with you," Vin said heartily. "I'm waked half to death, to coin a phrase."

"I'm on my way to a girl. And under the circumstances four would be rather a crowd."

It was the one excuse they would be able to find no way around. As he turned to leave, he saw a flash of envy cross Vin's face, and held-in, baffled rage on Garrett's.

It was after nine, long past Dr. Robert Littauer's consulting hours. He had sounded puzzled and a little irritated over the phone when Jack asked if he might see him briefly.

The Littauer house, handsome, modern, great sheets of glass and rough concrete, curves and decks and adventurous angles, was set back from the road leading to Race Point; Jack assessed it at an easy $175,000.

Have to tread softly, here; Dr. Littauer would have a lot at stake. He had hoped for a cozy talkative small-town man with a face or a voice you might be able to read. Instead, he got a tall balding worldly man with protuberant gray eyes, an air of money, authority, and a touch of annoyed impatience, opening the gleaming stainless-steel front door to him.

"Evening, Converse," he said. "We'll go into my study."

Jack followed him into the starkly white but comfortably furnished room, expecting at any moment to be told to strip and, now, let's see what's wrong with you.

Littauer leaned against a white desk, arms folded. His visitor was not invited to sit down.

"I believe Phip told me you're with the *Times*, am I right?"

"Yes, but that has nothing to do with—"

"Mmmmm." Littauer cut across him as though about to deliver a superior opinion on somebody's case. "What is it you wanted to ask me about?"

He felt invisible bindings around his arms. Important unsaid things said themselves, not projected by the composed Littauer but inside his own head.

Just barely mention malpractice—carelessness, a late partying summer night, a too permissive signing of the death certificate, and I'll have you in court. And if you think, my dear

young man, that I'm going to risk any slur on my practice if,
Wednesday morning, when the festive mists cleared, and I
shaved and showered, I had second thoughts about my patient's
death, the look on his face, the position of the body—

His own prepared lines came out easily enough. "I don't
like to take up your time, but I'd been due for a visit here the
night my uncle died and couldn't at the last minute make it,
and I've been blaming myself and wondering if—"

"If the pleasure of your company might have saved his life?"
Littauer smiled faintly. "Odd, you know, you don't look like
the soul-searching sentimentalist. Not at all. And you're my
second Converse today."

To the lifted eyebrows, he explained, "Garrett. I'd met him
before, in fact treated him for a virus when he was visiting
Phip several years ago—interesting man. We had a pleasant
chat, exchanged recollections of your uncle."

"Yes. But about Tuesday night."

"I am," the doctor said, "to put your conscience to rest. Is
that why you're here?"

Even considering that that was exactly why he was here, a
strangely accurate question, strangely put; but this man facing
him offered no handholds up his particular cliff.

"Yes," Jack said. "How did he . . . look? Do you think
there was much suffering—"

"A bit startled," Littauer said. "But then, death is the great
startler, isn't it. He looked, Converse, exactly the way a man
with a bad heart looks when his heart catches up with him. In
fact, he's had a better run for his money than he or I could
have hoped for."

Continuing in his role as the sentimentalist, and to hell with
what Littauer thought about it, he took a slight risk.

"When you went into his bedroom, did you have any impression that he'd had company during the evening? Mrs. Grahn
was out—a couple of glasses, mashed butts in the ashtray,
anything like that?" Stare answering stare, he added, "It would
be nice to think he wasn't alone, on his last night. Phip liked
company."

"I was entirely taken up with my patient; I don't recall
musing about his social life."

"When did he die? I know you can't pinpoint it but—"

"Between ten and midnight, give or take a quarter hour or so either way." He looked at his watch. "And now, I hope your mind is eased. . . ."

"Thank you very much, Doctor."

How sober were you when you at last made it to Phip's bedside, Dr. Littauer?

Doctors aren't all that unlike other people, are they: when they see something they expect to see they don't necessarily question it, do they.

You must have a fantastic practice here, Doctor, especially among the big money that you don't see on the streets of Provincetown, the big money hidden in the hills and behind the dunes—you wouldn't want to risk a cent of it, would you.

Ideas that couldn't be voiced by the layman, and especially by the reporter; questions that wouldn't be answered. Ever.

One thing was certain. If Mrs. Grahn's God ordered her to air her suspicions in public, deliver an explicit accusation of murder, Littauer would offer, in calm professional denial of anything she had to say, the same impenetrable shining surface as his stainless-steel front door.

And, he thought, getting back into the Ford, and giving the door a sudden savage slam that caught him by surprise, it hadn't been an entirely fruitless visit.

Garrett Converse was not given to idle reminiscing sessions with people he barely knew; he was a formal man, conscious of the value of his presence, and of his every minute. And he was not running for anything. And this was Massachusetts, not New York.

"We had a pleasant chat."

Garrett, of course, checking as his nephew had, to see if Phip's doctor, so far discreetly silent, suspected anything wrong. Fatally wrong.

ELEVEN

He told himself that his last stop, on impulse, before heading home was just a matter of common sense, thoroughness; Mr. Spiggott might, daunted by Leo's brusqueness and finger-tapping impatience, have hurried and shortened his story, left out a significant point or two.

At the back of his mind another, ridiculous reason hovered, and he promptly dismissed it: to see if the certified public accountant turned naturalist was still alive and well.

Perhaps Vin with his murderous tailgating—"Can't you take a joke?"—had given rise to this unreasonable fancy. Or Garrett, "You'd be too easy a target. . . ."

He wondered if Garrett carried a gun, in his attaché case; there had been several almost routine, in his Washington world, threats on his life in the past two or three years.

He stopped the Ford at a lighted telephone booth and looked up Spiggott, Thomas G., and found that he lived on Commercial Street at a number that should be directly across from the Flagship.

He knew the building, an old house divided up into apartments now; and he knew one of the tenants.

A small buzzer system beside the front door identified Spiggott's apartment as 2A. He knew 2B, to the right of it. He looked up at the left-hand apartment and saw its windows dark, and pressed the button of 2B.

Instead of immediately answering the buzzer, Jule Remond

pattered barefooted out onto the upper porch, peered down, saw him under the streetlight, and cried rapturously, *"Jacques!"* and then buzzed violently.

When she opened her door to him, she threw herself into his arms.

"Mon cher!"

"Ma chère!"

She was a tiny slender woman in her sixties with gray hair cut short around her small head, snapping dark eyes, and skin a permanent deep leathery gold from the Cape sun. She was head waitress at the Flagship. Jack had known her for at least a dozen years. Out of long affection, he kissed her warmly.

"It's obviously your night off and I won't keep you, Jule, your feet are probably in hell." Jule's feet had been a mutual topic for a decade.

"I'll lie down again as soon as I finish making love to you," Jule said. "You are looking, I may say, a bit *marr*-velously dark and dangerous." Still the unconquerable flirt, she ruffled spidery fingers through his hair. "What is it you want of Jule, my darling?"

"I was actually looking for Mr. Spiggott. Does he go to sleep this early?"

"No, no, the poor devil doesn't sleep well, he's out most nights very late, sometimes he's not home until morning, with any other man you might think he . . ."

She giggled. "But not Spiggott. Imagine a man in love with a tree, with a marsh, what a waste. And between my allergies, mon cher, and his pollens and dusts, he has the most terrible effect on me, fond of him as I am—I call him my Mr. Sneeze, but I think it amuses him."

Her mobile face changed and suddenly and sincerely became a mask of sorrow.

"But here I am laughing, and my poor sweet Mr. Converse is dead, the good God bless and keep him."

Jack thought that, if encouraged, she would reminisce. ". . . Mon Dieu, the tips, the parties, tables for six, eight, ten, and then champagne ordered for us girls afterward, all of us . . ." and she would also weep extravagantly. He decided he couldn't, at the moment, take it; he might weep himself.

He gave her a quick hug. "I have to be off, Jule. If he comes in before you go to sleep or if you see him in the morning, will you ask him to get in touch with me?"

And then on an afterthought, trusting her, "What's all the gossip, that Min was whispering to me about?"

"Whenever there's a man alone with a woman, and money for a pinch of salt, they'll talk," Jule said, and winked, and added, "My own grandfather, on the Gaspé, had an affair of the heart with his nurse, at eighty-nine, and left her all his hens and cows, and his house, and his money, but they were a blind lazy lot, the sons and daughters, thinking it would all come to them as the sun rises and sets." She gave him a light Gallic tap on the side of his nose. "I'll be coming out to Truro to see Mr. Converse tomorrow if I won't be in the way."

"Of course not—now go put your feet up."

"Until then, le beau Jacques . . . ," ending with a phrase he thought odd, and penetrating, "good hunting, mon cher."

Nobody followed murderously close behind him on the twisting narrow hilly road home to North Truro.

Vin's car was no longer parked across the street from the Flagship, but it might have found its way to other places of food and drink and reassuring racket, the Moors, the Atlantic House, Mike's.

His own bedroom was one of the three over the garage, Vin and Glenna's across the hallway, Garrett's the deeply eaved larger room at the back, the few extra yards of space befitting the dignity of a senator, if not the skull-cracking slant of the roof.

Timothy, when and if he was in bed, was accommodated at a motel a quarter of a mile away. Leo was staying at the house of friends of his and Phip's, in Truro. Jack didn't know what Tike's arrangements were; perhaps the man in the MG was a part of them.

He thought about Sophie, Marcia, and Kate with their bedrooms in the main house. About Kate in particular.

Too bad there wasn't a man in the house, except the quiet man in the coffin. But, again, ridiculous. The moon so bright, the night so mild and calm with just the occasional pour of wind from the sea, like clean salty water.

Marcia, as he remembered from earliest childhood, could be more formidable than a commissioner of police. And attempting some sort of mischief against Sophie, tall soft-voiced tough Sophie, would be a thing you would have to think about twice.

Kate, though.

He had no slightest idea about how good Kate was at taking care of herself.

The front door of the house was unlocked. The door to Phip's office was closed, light coming from under it; he smelled Leo's pipe tobacco. The dining room had one low lamp burning, every trace of the feast cleared away, the table surface softly shining. The smell of flowers from the living room was a kind of drug. He went in to throw all four windows wide open.

And then, without troubling to examine his motives, he went up the steep short staircase.

Marcia's door, to the left, was closed, no light on. Sophie's room, directly in front of him, was dark and empty. Kate's door on his right was open three or four inches. Neither a forbidding nor an inviting door; a family sort of aperture.

He stood outside it, and might not have gone in at all if he hadn't heard the faint sound, like the faraway cry of a sea gull; peculiarly helpless, coming from a human throat.

Opening the door very quietly, he went in. Through drawn rose-colored curtains, in a sweeping, steady heartbeat, Highland Light illumined the room every sixty seconds.

She was lying with her back to him, and he was astonished to see that the hair swathed so softly and casually about her head in waking hours was long, falling almost to her waist.

Perhaps he had only imagined that the gull cry came from within the room. But then, as she half turned on her back, it came again, high, thin, a half gasp. And, "No—no—*Ferdie*—"

Phip crying, "No, oh no—" to Mr. Spiggott's ears. Perhaps Phip too had been dreaming, after all. But this sound chilled him.

Kate was dreaming that she was standing at the altar beside Ferdie di Castro, all in white, the veil over her face clouding her vision, and she thought, This is mad, corny, I never wanted a white wedding—but the altar step they now knelt down on was the velvet kneeler beside Phip's coffin and there he lay, with a bishop-looking figure beyond in a lace smock-like garment, hands raised in blessing—them? or Phip?—shadowy, on the far side of the coffin. It was wrong, all wrong, the veil, and being married, it must be over, the ceremony, if they were being blessed, and it was too late, something had been irretrievably lost, and what, oh what, was she to do.

She swung a groping hand out over the edge of the bed.

After a second's hesitation, Jack took the hand as lightly and carefully as he knew how to touch human flesh.

In a way, she terrified him. It was indecent to intrude on these immense privacies; but then, in the flight of her dreams, a Mars distance away, she might want the anchoring unknown hand, need it. He stayed still.

Perhaps it was the contact, however delicate, that stopped the whispered cries. She lay breathing quietly and then her lashes stirred.

"No"—the voice somewhere halfway back from sleep—"Ferdie."

"Not Ferdie," he murmured. "Me. Jack. Don't be frightened"—as she started wide awake, defensively seized her sheet to her chin, recognized him in a fan of light, standing over her, and let out a long sigh.

"What on earth?" She sat up, braced.

"I was making my rounds, a self-appointed night watchman, and I heard you cry out when I was on the landing. A bad dream—I didn't want to wake you and scare you out of it, so . . ."

Her hand was still in his. He released it and placed it gently on the sheet, and bent and kissed her as he might kiss a child recovering from distress, on her damp forehead. "Go back to sleep now, Kate, you'll be all right . . . good night."

In a surprised rush, she said, "Thank you—that was very kind, and sweet—I was in such a mess and then I had a feeling someone had come to help me. . . ."

Ferdie, he thought.

No. *Me*. Jack.

A light sprang up on the landing, the door was pushed open, and Marcia, in a tailored dark blue bathrobe, stood in the doorway, demanding, "What is going on here?"

Exactly, Jack thought, like an outraged housemother.

Over the unexpected blaze of guilt she inspired in him—seeming to be caught about to attempt something frightful right under her nose—he had a wild impulse to shout with laughter.

He saw a faint flickering around Kate's eyes and mouth and sensed she was on the brink of mirth too.

"I was having a horrible dream," she explained, "and flailing around and shouting for help like a madwoman and he heard and naturally came to see what he could do about it."

"*I* heard no shouts and flailing. My door was closed, of course, but even then—"

Her crisp disapproving voice, from another generation and another world, suggested to all three of them without her intending to do so the unspeakable behavior she might have fortunately interrupted just in time, the two bodies, her niece's and her nephew's, uncaringly and delightedly locked, and her brother downstairs, among his flowers and candles and mass cards, dead.

She removed herself forcibly from the scene she had projected. "But then, it's been a bad day for all of us, a very bad day. If you're nervous and upset, Kate, I have aspirin in my room."

"*Aspirin!*"

The joy, the blessedness of being pulled back, by a hand, from final and impossible mistakes, disasters; and then the schoolgirl feeling of being one great blush from head to foot under Marcia's basilisk glare. . . .

She couldn't help herself, but burst into a cascade of laughter.

Jack's hand went to her shoulder and tightened on it and helped stop the laughing, which had, she knew, a flying edge of hysteria.

"Sorry, a bit giddy, it's so nice to know it all wasn't really happening. Thank you, I have aspirin of my own—and good night to both of you, I hope I won't disturb you further."

"I'll leave my door open," Marcia said. "In case you're troubled again."

Does she mean that, Jack said to himself, going down the stairs, and finally allowing himself to shake a little with his own silent laughter, as a threat or a promise?

And wondered, going out through the front door, what Leo was doing in the little office, behind the closed door.

Leo had taken a good hour over his methodical search of Phip's desk and filing cabinet. Only his duty, he assured himself, and a tiresome chore indeed. There were letters and snapshots and postcards and seed catalogues, and mysterious figurings of enormous sums on scratch paper. There was a large photograph of Jack's mother, Eve, delightfully fair and caught up in laughter, before John Anthony Converse's death—hidden away like this, why? Well, yes—Phip had been for a time in love with her himself. And matchbooks, newspaper clippings, an essay of Jack's, written at the age of thirteen, about a day he had spent beginning at dawn with the Province-town fishing fleet. A good precise eye even then. A disturbingly observant young man.

And a pair of square-cut topaz cuff links of their father's, over which they had had a mild battle eighteen years ago. "You borrowed them and never returned them—" "I did so." "You did not."

There was nothing, among the papers, of or from Mrs. Grahn. Just one snapshot of the two of them sitting on the white iron lace settee, Phip joining her in shelling peas and grinning like a boy about it.

His eyebrows shot upward as he examined papers from a thin red legal envelope. Two days before his brother's death developers had picked up a then unlikely piece of land, one thousand acres, that Phip had bought on Staten Island in 1950; the developers were prepared to pay $1,200,000. At the bottom of the offering letter, Phip had written to himself, "Okay I think, send to Leo."

He sighed heavily. Yes, a distressing amount of property, money, not even counting this unexpected find—like a new gold field discovered under Arctic ice—to be frozen in litigation. But, of course, you could mine or bomb ice away, to get comfortably at your gold.

TWELVE

Mrs. Grahn impatiently scoured French chocolate icing out of a heavy pot, her tenth pot tonight, to say nothing of the pans and silver and glasses and mountains of dishes.

Scrubbing, rinsing, drying, putting away for a pack of Converses, evil in their midst, partying in a house whose heart had stopped.

Unable in spite of herself to be careless, reckless, with Mr. Converse's beautiful things, she tenderly dried an airy yellow and white Belleek pitcher.

Shelving china, separating spoons and forks and knives, she thought about what else she would be putting away. Her own bedroom upstairs, the room that Sophie woman would sleep in tonight. The long stiff white chintz curtains patterned with green vines, the thick green rug that melted under your toes. The big bed covered in the viny chintz, quilted; a great white taffeta down-filled puff folded across its foot. She had fallen into the habit of decking the room with flowers. There was usually a fat cut-crystal pitcher of them on the pretty little green-enameled dressing table.

While she'd be in bed, reading her nice magazines, *Woman's Day* and *Family Circle*, hunting for recipes he might enjoy, she would hear from below, not at all loud, wonderfully soothing really, his records on his phonograph, new sounds to her ear, Mozart, Bach, Beethoven, interspersed with Ella Fitzgerald and Count Basie and his beloved Billie Holiday. The late Mr.

Grahn had been a devotee of Lawrence Welk.

Her seldom used room and her sister's in Provincetown, the spare room, was small and narrow. There was a suite of shiny pine furniture, a single bed covered in white chenille, an oval rag rug, a beige crocheted runner on the dresser, centered with a bouquet of bright pink plastic roses.

She bent, put a hand to the small of her back, and slowly straightened up.

She had kept pushing it away, obscuring it with hard work these past few days, not really facing it. Everything, all of it, stopped, gone, stolen from her.

And when the wake and burying were over there would be another burial, her house, her world. Its contents no doubt seized by the family share and share alike, its curtains taken down, refrigerator and magnificently stocked pantry emptied ("I'd suggest you see that any food supplies left go to the hospital," Marcia Dalrymple had said crisply). Floors given a final scrubbing, windows washed, doors locked, from the outside. And then the FOR SALE sign on the front lawn, an indecency.

As she looked around her warm and immaculate kitchen, Pitch curled asleep on a side shelf of the black iron stove, the termination hit her in full force.

Something had to be done. They couldn't be allowed to get away with it.

She had for a time found a certain heady pleasure in her own indecision. A mysterious sense of something at her command; power withheld, waiting. The way they looked at her, watching, intent, whenever she walked into a room on the most prosaic of errands. She felt following her everywhere the hot exhilarating glow of the spotlight. It was strangely gratifying to be, to these glistening daunting people, almost as important a personage in the house as the man in the coffin.

But soon . . . Rest in peace, Mr. Philip Andrew Converse. The family to harvest in peace, spend in peace.

Over and above her loss and her anger, and the war of helplessness against vengeance, there had been circling a sharp immediate curiosity about Mr. Spiggott's visit.

From the kitchen window she had seen him come to the front

door. Opening her kitchen door, ears alert, she had heard him
asking if there was someone he could have a few words in
private with.

She'd wanted to listen at the closed door of the office but
was afraid that someone would come and find her at it.

She knew him to say hello to, to exchange the time of day
with. A shy man, keeping himself to himself. Why on earth
did he want to see a Converse in private? You saw people alone
when you had things to say that other people mustn't be allowed
to hear. Secrets.

Perhaps there might be some help, for her, in Mr. Spiggott's
secrets.

There was no answer when at the wall phone near the pantry
she dialed his number. Probably prowling the night woods and
fields in his odd way. He'd be home later, heaven knew how
much later; but bone-tired as she was, she felt the pressure of
things to be done, time getting short, an urgency catching at
her, making it hard to breathe.

She put on her good black coat—at least one person could
wear proper mourning for him, those people in their expensive
festive clothes—and went out and got into her car.

She was surprised and pleased to find Mr. Spiggott's old
dark red Chevrolet parked at the crossroads, pulled well off to
one side. No time like the present, Mrs. Grahn informed herself.
Catch him before you slept. You never knew what tomorrow
would bring.

Perhaps this was the Sign she had been waiting for, con-
fusedly hoping and praying for.

Following an instinct of caution she neither understood nor
examined, she parked her own car in the driveway of an un-
tenanted house halfway up the hill, walked back to the crossroads, and opened Mr. Spiggott's car door, which had been
left trustingly locked. She placed herself behind the wheel,
and waited.

Tonight, Mr. Spiggott supposed, sleep would be even more
elusive.

The sight of the dead man, serene, unreal, had distressed
him deeply. His nostrils were haunted by a towering basket

that had crowded too closely on him, crimson roses and white lilacs, where did people find white lilacs in October?

A mile, or two, or three would help. And perhaps the sea air would clean away the scent, and the memory of the scent. He found himself broodingly glad that he had left strict orders with his sister that he be cremated.

The night clouds were heavy, the light of the moon obscure, diffused. He heard a faint thumping noise quite near, behind him, and was alarmed for a moment; but it was only a very large noisy rabbit.

The fleeting sense of danger now innocently dispersed bothered Mr. Spiggott. In a world that seemed to him increasingly savage, unlivable, he cherished the peace he found in woods and meadows and moors, where the small violences—of animals, birds, rodents—were unplanned and in their way natural and necessary, and certainly not undertaken for profit, but for survival.

He got out his pipe and lit it. The match flame reminded him of Leo Converse tense with something, having only measured-out split seconds to spare, hearing him out in his dark-browed saturnine way. Very inhibiting. He recalled Queen Victoria's statement to her husband, Albert, when kept a moment or so beyond her time of expecting him, ''We almost had to wait.'' From his certified public accountant days he responded still to the might and power of Leavings, Radnor, Currie and Converse, up in their eagle heights on Wall Street, above black little Trinity Church. It made him feel small, and time-wasting, and dithery.

There were other things, if he had been given time to do so, organize his thoughts, that he had wanted to say.

The anonymous parked car thrust in under willows eighty yards or so down the road, no one in it, not even, to his timid passing glance, a half-concealed boy and girl—

The cat Pitch's thin lifting cry, as though in vague pain or ancient woe.

A smell, close to the window, nothing to do with the herb garden or the scents and savors of the house. Exotic grasses from the East, a touch of peppermint and jasmine . . . a sweat-soaked sweetness, Mr. Spiggott described it to himself, indelicate, he added, as that might sound.

And something he had caught his shoe in on the front doorstep, a silk scarf or handkerchief, he didn't know which. He had stuffed it into his pocket without thinking much about the gesture. Now, which clothes had he been wearing that night?

Prodded by Jule Remond, he had handed a dump of things to the laundry and cleaning man when his sheets were brought back on Wednesday. Trousers, a jacket or maybe two, shirts. The scarf might have been included.

But there were no words to describe, even if given time, the real upheaval, to Leo Converse; the atavistic sense of nearby encroaching doom, which had made him curl into himself, protectively, praying he would be spared.

His sister Hester appeared in ghostly fashion, although she was very much alive in New Bedford. "Indigestion, Thomas, you and your fancies. You will insist on eating fried potatoes and onions. Take one half teaspoon of bicarbonate of soda in a full glass of water. Immediately."

Leo Converse reared before him, tall and dark and threatening as some apocalyptic figure in a dream, courtroom voice muted and dangerous: "What is it that you're suggesting? If anything?"

Interference. A word out of his childhood, used by a kindly delicate father to his wife in front of a small timid boy. A woman—ah—interfered with. A man more or less accidentally dying in his own lumberyard, the sister and the wife, well, you know, dear, all those two-by-fours, a mountain of them tumbling on him, I'd be inclined to say, interference. . . .

The closest he had been able to come to the truth in the Converse house was that he thought someone had interfered with Mr. Converse. Although of course he hadn't said it, at all.

Troubled, pushing away a half-conceived idea, he turned to his left and went down a slope through long grass, brambles catching at his trousers, to the narrow road. It was one of his favorite spots in North Truro, an old choked canal on the bay side of the main road, scrub and woodland beyond that. On the near side of the canal, set in coarse grass, was a bronze plaque mounted on a small unassuming piece of granite, which he always stopped to read with pleasure and affection: "On this spot the Pilgrims spent their second night in the New World.''

The idea wouldn't go away. What if someone in Philip Converse's own family had interfered with him? He had heard, without listening seriously to it, the speculation, the stories about the woman who took care of him; but then some people thought *he* was wooing Jule, Jule with her sore feet, and always sneezing.

Time to go home. "Thomas," his sister said, close by, "get to bed. Have some hot milk and crackers, they'll help."

As he was approaching his car, headlights from another car coming down the hill caught the Chevrolet briefly and without any kind of accuracy to Mr. Spiggott's eyes, shortsighted behind inadequate glasses. Bifocals, he had long since said to himself, *never*.

Somebody sitting at the wheel of his car. A dark bulking figure. Motionless. Waiting.

He had never really known what Shakespeare meant, in his famous line; but now not only this thumbs but his fingertips pricked with an immediate and instinctive physical fear.

Standing, as he had, in the doorway of a roomful of people. Exposed and naked. The faces made a composite, all fierce blue eyes and threatening aquiline nose. But of course there had been a softness here and there, women, a girl you might come upon in the woods and exchange a word or so with, a dappled sort of girl. . . .

If anything unpleasant, unfortunate, had happened in the house, he would have been seen before tonight by one possessor of those composite eyes. Seen waiting at the front door, listening, hoping and praying everything was all right within, trying to swallow down the feeling of disaster.

Walk to the car door, fling it open, say, What are you doing in my automobile? Breath short and bones quailing, he thought, well, maybe on television—

Get a bus to Provincetown and leave the car here? There wouldn't be another bus through for an hour and a half.

Thumb a ride? People were rightfully careful about picking up people these days. A middle-aged woman stopping for a jeaned boy last month had been raped and murdered and tossed into an innocent blue pond near Orleans.

Go back to the lighted Converse house and stay until his car was emptied of its alien presence? Ask that man, that younger man, to walk down the road with him to the car—

Why? the young man would ask. What are you afraid of, what are you suggesting?

His mind, without sorting out reactions, rejected this solution.

In the end, he turned to his natural retreat, and his safety and his home, the moors and the sea. An hour or two in the silvered crystal dark air would be nothing. Refreshing, reassuring. And whoever it was in the car would tire and go away to where he or she slept. For tonight, anyway.

Indigestion, Thomas. You and your fancies.

For the second time in fifteen minutes, he paused and lit his pipe, observing in the brief glow a young owl intent on an unseen mouse.

I shouldn't, he thought nervously, be lighting myself up, like a firefly; and he made a stamping sound on the grass, to warn the mouse away from a little death in the night.

THIRTEEN

"Always a ghastly task," Marcia said, red spots flaming on her cheekbones, "but someone's got to do it."

It was Jack's turn, if not his intention, to embarrass his aunt.

In his room over the garage, the idea of sleep had kept retreating. One of the windows faced the house across the road, the other looked to the sea, and as the white sweeping cone from the lighthouse bestowed its by now overly wakeful signals, he found himself responding to it, the sweep, the beat, in a most peculiar way.

An almost unidentifiable late night feeling, some sort of emotional knee jerk, Highland Light being the rubber hammer.

An extraordinary bounding happiness just out of reach and not to be catalogued, a promise, something deep, stirring, something beginning.

Fatigue, probably. To bed at three, after an unwillingly attended but necessary party, and after willing and necessary Eugenia. Then up, in the unfamiliar morning dark, a memorable ride to the airport that was much too fast and accident-prone, the driver huddled over his wheel and moaning after he had gone through a red light, "Jeez, these cramps—it must be all that rum I drank." The short flight from Washington to Boston, burnt English muffins and watery coffee at Logan, and from there a little orange four-seater plane with a cargo of sea worms on the two back seats. The pilot, a boy who appeared mildly deranged, had said, when they were coming in to land at

Provincetown, "Would you mind looking out your window to see if there's anything coming at us, the radio's zonked—"

And mourning was a tiring business. To say nothing about drinks piled upon drinks.

He switched on the bedside lamp for the third time and put on a robe and walked the room restlessly. Mr. Spiggott bothered him, wandering in, in his innocence and ignorance, wanting a few words in private.

They had all seen him. They had all heard him. He found himself wishing he had been able to place Mr. Spiggott securely in his apartment, browsing over his notes on herbs and flowers or better still safely in bed.

He went to the window and leaned on the sill and stared at the house across the road, the house with its own life and its own secrets. A dim light was coming from the back room, sending out mothy wings on either side. So quiet. So unlikely-looking as a source, a breeding ground, of possible deadly danger, for someone.

The radio on the bedside table, turned low, muttered disaster at him: ". . . burned to death in their house on Bleecker Street. . . . A man suffering a heart attack in the Lincoln Tunnel caused a six-car pileup in which three people were critically injured. . . . A young woman has been found strangled to death on a park bench in Washington Square, tentatively identified as Katherine Con—"

Her surname was interrupted by the lightning snapping off of the sound. Thanks a lot, WQXR, Radio Station of the New York *Times*.

For God's sake get to bed, to sleep. Or be flown away with by fancies.

The thin demanding wail that tensed his fingertips on the windowsill puzzled him for a second or two; a determined repeated sound.

The black cat, Pitch. Someone must have locked him out, by design or accident, and he was now asking for entrance at the front door. He had always slept at the foot of Phip's bed. Jack remembered him as being a single-minded animal. Swearing mildly to himself, he went down the outside stairs and crossed the street and unlocked the front door. He felt rather than saw the black against black of the cat, a velvet glide past his bare leg.

Was it Sophie who was still up? He went through the living room and, without knocking, opened the door into the back room.

The first thing he saw, in the light of one low lamp, was a twist of paper hurled accurately through the air into the heart of the smoldering fire. There was a brief consuming pale flare.

The leopard bed was covered with garments, Phip's. There were no closets in the room; Phip had kept his clothes in an immense old armoire, dully green lacquered, mirror-paneled and painted with faded flamingos, which he had found in Paris. The door toward Jack was open, and underneath it he saw the hem of a pink nightgown, stockings, and walking shoes.

"Marcia?"

She looked uncharacteristically nervous and guilty. ". . . someone's got to do it."

He looked at his watch. "But at two o'clock—"

"Of course, having waked all the world, Kate's fast asleep now," she said tartly, her eyes defying him to find anything strange about this early morning ferreting through her brother's clothing. "*I* haven't closed an eye since, so I thought I'd make myself useful. I don't imagine that you want any of these things—you're bigger than he was, taller. Some deserving charity . . ."

"No. I suppose you're going through all the pockets as a matter of course." She flushed again at the clear statement in his gaze: ghastly task, hell, you're looking for something, or looking to be sure there isn't something, having to do with Mrs. Stella Grahn. What had been burned, just now?

She went on rapidly, "Phip was always frightfully careless about leaving things in his pockets. I was once up here, sending things to the cleaner's, and just in time saved a check for nine hundred dollars. And in another suit, a crumpled-up fifty-dollar bill. . . ."

"A treasure hunt, then," he said.

The latent grande dame surfaced, and "You're being impertinent, Jack!" she said. "Get back to bed and let me get on with it and try to get some sleep myself—but with the comings and goings in this house, and the radio, and the clumpings on the stairs . . .''

As he contemplated her serviceable walking shoes, she added, "I do *not* myself clump. —I heard a noise out in back, under my window, and got a flashlight and went out, it was a large dog, a German pointer, I believe, trying to push open the lid of the garbage bin, I shooed him off."

Her voice faded; she looked weary, used up. It was not like crisp commanding Marcia to offer these small explanations.

Feeling the immense silence, the stillness, from the next room, he responded to it and went and put an arm around her thin shoulders and lightly kissed her cheek.

"To borrow your phraseology, you are to go to bed this instant," he said. "I'll finish up here."

"Yes, Jack." Unexpectedly disarming as a child.

He found nothing, in his rapid painful exploration of tweeds and cashmeres, flannels and worsteds, but paper matchbooks, fresh linen handkerchiefs, a British halfpenny, and a roll of indigestion tablets. Breathing faintly over all, Phip's custom-blended cologne, suggesting apples and heather; a memorial scent.

"I mean, if it turned out to be true," the man said, "not that we're not both well known right now, but, sweetie, we'd be a household word. I don't believe anyone has ever *touched* this kind of thing."

He was Robbin Roy, the photographer, whose plane had rocked Phip's house and family. By now he had had a great deal to drink but, although driving fast, he handled the MG neatly and well. The hover of danger, the tear of speed intensified by the openness of the car, pleased and in a way soothed Tike.

After a moment she said, "I don't know . . . yes, why not, it's okay with me, crazy, man. . . ."

Precipices were exciting.

She was quite sober herself. She was her own intoxication and needed no fuel.

"But remember," she said as at her direction he stopped the MG several hundred yards down the road from the house, "quiet. As a mouse. As the grave," and surprised herself into a giggle.

Both the house and the garage were dark. The moon had vanished. It was a little before four in the morning.

Someone, though—at *their* ages—might be sleepless, might be up, watching and listening.

"Give me your hand," Tike murmured. "You've—got your camera?"

"Has Columbus got his compass?" he muttered back indignantly. "Has Astaire got his tails?" He patted the Rolleiflex on his hip, hanging by its leather strap.

Gracefully sure of every step, Tike guided him up the road, through the hedge opening, and across the grass to the front door.

Nothing squeaked or groaned in this well-run house, except an occasional old plank underfoot; the key in the lock was soundless. They stood just inside the door, in the hall, listening.

Music played very faintly from above, Rachmaninoff's *Isle of the Dead*. Not knowing what she was hearing, Tike thought it was gloomy. Either someone was awake or they had fallen asleep with their radio on. Was this or wasn't it a good idea?

Another high thrilling precipice.

Through the dining room, into the living room. The candles at either end of the coffin had been extinguished. They waited while their eyes adjusted to the darkness; shapes began to proclaim themselves dimly.

The flowers possessed the air, the room, the night. Some sudden stir of wind struck a basket of white chrysanthemums, loosened petals, and tossed them to the floor, and the delicate rustle jolted Robbin Roy.

For a second he wondered what the hell, after all, he was doing here. Then, briskly, he collected himself and flicked up the lid of the Rolleiflex with a thumbnail.

"One real grieving shot, just in case," had been his first suggestion, in the MG. "And then far, far out. Who knows? Anything goes, these days."

The faraway music was beginning to make him nervous.

"Now," Tike whispered.

Faint click of the shutter and blue lightning of the flash.

Grieving shot, kneeling, but with profile to the camera. Within seconds, another signal. White-satin Tike seated on the edge of the coffin, her uncle's face rosily visible beyond her hand, a tower of palms in tubs as a backdrop.

Terrific, Robbin Roy thought, my God, terrific. He was going to have to leave it to her from here, the choice of poses; but she had a feeling for these things.

Another shot, sitting pensively on the kneeler, her back to the coffin, facing him, in the immediate foreground a tall half-obscuring white vase of calla lilies and babies'-breath.

"One more," Tike whispered.

She bent and put her lips to her Uncle Phip's forehead. In a way the best shot of all, her body one shining streak of horror as she felt the iciness, the marble, the truth of death.

He got another one of her appalled recoil before there was the sound from the doorway. Before a lamp was switched on and the room went warmly golden.

"Jesus," Timothy said. "Jesus."

Still feeling the stain of ice on her lips that might stay there forever, Tike clutched at life, at recovery, at nerve.

"Not really, in spite of the pretty gold beard," she said. "Actually, it's Robbin Roy. Rob: my brother, Timothy—I don't think you've met."

Timothy was still fully dressed, in his cream-colored suit. He looked thin, ghostlike, staring at them from the doorway.

"Not that it's any of your business, but I wanted some last pictures of Uncle Phip to remember him by," Tike said coolly. "And what are you doing here at this hour? Looking for a flower for your buttonhole, or something?"

"I've heard of people dancing on other people's graves," Tomothy said in a remote voice, "but not— What are you trying for? The cover of the *Mortuary Monthly*?"

Robbin Roy's scotches were beginning to catch up with him in earnest. He could have sworn he heard Tike say, fast, low, and blurred, "I just had the most wonderful idea. We'll confess to it, and say we did it, together, you wanted the money so you could get on with your painting, and I was afraid—my side of it—that I'd be, next year or the year after, just, sort of, crap, used up, finished, so we made this pact. . . . And then the police will move in and clear us and prove it wasn't true. And all those men in the black robes and white wigs—''

She was a devotee of late night movies and had her own clear picture of lawyers and mysterious things like probate.

''—will say, no question, then, split up the money and enjoy yourselves. That ought to get rid of Mrs. Ghoul or whatever her name is, for good. She wanted a murder and we gave her one and it turned out that it hadn't happened at all.''

''And you'd make the papers,'' Timothy said. ''And they could use whatever pictures have been taken here. No thank you. Even though the death penalty is more or less up in the air, I don't think I want to play, Tike. Especially as, the way you put it, it sounds sort of convincing.'' Brother and sister exchanged a glance of blood knowledge of each other. ''And so, with a witness present''—he studied Robbin Roy's heavy eyelids and half-glazed stare—''a sort of one, anyway . . . In case there are any spoons missing, or corpses found, new ones, I came over here from the motel to get a book to see me through to coffee, I couldn't sleep.''

''You have, as it happens, two witnesses,'' Sophie said softly, immediately behind him. ''Interestin' listenin' around here.''

Tike started violently. Robbin Roy, with a feeling that things were coming apart, and a sudden sense of guilt, said, ''Well, session's over, want to go out and carouse some more, Tike, or—''

''No,'' Tike said. ''Just drive us home to bed. But first— okay, Sophie, I can use two witnesses too. Rob and I have been bar-crawling, on and off, and I've been hearing things, people talking behind their hands, maybe it's true, what Mrs. Grahn said. Y'all might be interested to know Sophie's business is in big bad trouble and she could use a hunk of money and she's down the drain without it.''

Sophie made a great swooping move toward her and Timothy caught the soft, strong wrist.

He said, ''Get the hell out of here, Tike, you'll wake the house,'' and Tike, with one look at Sophie's face, seized Robbin Roy's hand and said, ''Got your camera? Yes, let's go.''

Sophie snatched her wrist from Timothy. '' '. . . You wanted the money so you could get on with your painting,' " she quoted. "And next year your sister'll be 'sort of crap.' A considerable understatement. 'So *we* made this pact.' "

"Is this aimed at me or at her?" he asked. She looked at him, through him, as though she wasn't seeing him at all, and turned to go back upstairs.

"It's started, hasn't it?" he said. "I mean, it's come out from under a rock and really started."

Sophie paused halfway up the stairs.

"Yes," she said, "it has, they've opened the pits and let the vipers out. Who killed Cock Robin . . . maybe? Everybody watch their own hats and coats, management not responsible, management happenin' to be deceased."

FOURTEEN

Anticipating a mild traffic jam in the morning, three bathrooms for seven people, Kate got up early, found she had been beaten to the one on the upper floor—someone's teeth, probably Marcia's, being brushed vigorously behind a closed door—and went down the steep shadowy steps and past the flowers, and Phip, to the door of the bathroom off the back room. She was a little taken aback to find that not twenty feet away from the coffin she could feel a normal indignation at another closed door, showering noises coming from within. Someone from across the street had most unfairly taken over this facility. She was sure Sophie was still asleep.

A door opened above and she went back up, to blue tiles and faint steam and a wet immaculate tub and Marcia's clean sharp cologne in the air.

Half an hour later, she made herself a cup of instant coffee in the big sunny empty kitchen and took it out to drink on the iron lace settee. The air stung sweetly, blue air, shining in the sun.

Jack found her there, in her slender water-green pants suit, the fresh keen light discovering amber and blue and violet in the wrapped dark hair.

Still warmed with her memory of being rescued by him, the night before, caught back from some disastrous brink, she smiled up at him and used in a warm soft voice a greeting from long ago, when she was fourteen or fifteen.

"Good morning, John Anthony."

He looked a little startled. "Good morning, Kate."

So much for unasked-for endearments, for reaching out a hand to touch, lightly, something that wasn't there at all.

She went a deep dark pink. It was like missing a step on a stairway.

There must be various Jack Converses he could produce at will, all of them attractive and authentic. He looked rested and glistening, a bit damp at his hairline, with soap and water; and exuding vigor, a relish in the air, in the morning, in himself. Even standing still, hands in his pockets, eyes on her, he seemed to be in motion.

Yes, amiable, good-natured, her cousin, attending their uncle's wake with her, ships passing, saluting politely, to more or less borrow his own words.

She thought she understood. He didn't need her comfort any more. He had found his balance.

She ate the pear she had taken from the bowl on the round oak table and finished her coffee.

"Now that you've consumed that Henry the Eighth repast," Jack said, "will you come Spiggott-hunting with me?"

He had gotten up from a short but deep sleep determined to deal, in this clear light of day, forthrightly and factually with everyone and everything.

It was more than time to brush away uncertainty, confusion, an enfolding cobweb, a foraging aunt burning possible evidence in a night fire, hysterical accusations from a red-haired trollop, a dark-hours sense of danger hanging over Mr. Spiggott's gray head; and a strange new disease connected with Kate that might be called Highland Light virus.

He was going, this morning, to ply his intelligence and wring the present, clear-cut, explainable, from all these mists.

And get himself, all of himself, back. To return free and clear to the graspable realities and demands and pleasures of work, and Washington, and Eugenia. Eugenia?

Even while he was making up his mind that this was the obvious, the only, direction, he found himself wondering, But which *is* reality?

Is the truth here, mystery, violence, murder, guilt, the drives of fear, of desperate need, or greed, or both, all with a warmth and shine somewhere near the center of it—Kate?

And the safeties and practicalities of daily life and work, beckoning to him, an escape, a deliberate closing of the eyes . . . ?

It would be a relief and in a way an answer of sorts when the final amen was said, over Phip.

What was Kate saying? ". . . whatever Spiggott-hunting is, yes, I'd like to get out of the house."

She had been tempted to refuse but thought it would appear, and accurately, a bit bruised, sulky.

Not wanting to alarm her, he said, "There are a couple of things I want to talk to him about and I can't reach him at his apartment, so we will stalk him through the woods and over the moors."

He withheld Jule Remond's information that, as far as she knew, he hadn't come home at all last night. His car, always parked in front, was not there. And that his telephone had rung, and rung again, annoyingly, late; and someone knocking at his door had waked her up still *again*, mon cher.

"Are we working for the *Times*, or for you?" Kate asked lightly.

"To paraphrase Garrett, you mean." He was cool. "No. In a way we're working for Spiggott."

"Well," Kate said, equally cool, "you're very mysterious, but in any case I can use the air and the exercise."

Jule had said that Truro and North Truro had been his beat for the last two or three months.

"First we'll have to find his car, and this may well be a wild Spiggott chase." They got into Jack's rented Ford. "He could be in Boston or visiting his relatives, if he had any, or have switched his attentions to Race Point or Dennis or Brewster."

They found his dark red Chevrolet more or less by chance. Kate was following the flight of a cardinal into the woods and caught a flash of sun on metal, a car driven into a shady rutted lane on the right.

"Probably not his, but let's look, can you turn around?"

It was his, empty, tidily parked, pulled well off the lane

although it looked to be unused. They got out of the Ford, into gold and green powerfully laced with the scent of pine.

Jack reached in through an open window and took out a pair of binoculars slung over the seat. "Just a loan, Mr. Spiggott."

"Let's split up," Kate said. "Would you mind the bay side? There are swamps beyond those woods, I remember, and I once stepped barefooted on a perfectly innocent big milk snake, but still . . . and I'll take the ocean."

"Split up? Why?"

"Twice as useful. On your paper, you don't go about in teams, do you?"

"My first view of the crisp efficient executive Kate," he said. "What happened to the blushing girl eating her pear under an aspen tree? I don't want to split up. There's the one remote chance that you might find something that—"

"Well, I do," Kate said. "We can't spend the whole morning on your wild Spiggott chase. I'll meet you back here at the car in, say, half an hour."

"All right, go waste your blushes on the moors, then."

She thought he was callous, unkind, amused at her, and was glad to be free of him, finding across the main road a path through scrub pine, rising, curving, and loosing her on the great liberating sprawl of the moors under the blue towering sky.

She saw a man in the distance, coming toward her. Vin. He raised a hailing arm and when they met gave her a hearty cousinly hug.

"Marvelous here, isn't it," he said. "I forgot what it feels like to be sprung from Manhattan, let out of jail for a day or so."

He looked terrible in the light of the minted morning, battered, weary, his skin all the wrong colors.

"Vin dear, don't you ever get to sleep at night?" She looked anxiously up, worried about him.

"*Sleep*. Christ, I sleep like the dead, my problem is waking up to greet the bright new day. Speaking of greeting the day, come on back with me, it's more than time for a Bloody Mary."

"Thanks, I need a good deal more walking—"

"Please, Kate? Please. I want your company. I miss you, I don't see enough of you any more."

She hesitated before his urgency, remembering his kindness,

his funniness, their shared laughter, their touchstone jokes. But
then, Jack couldn't be left dangling, looking at his watch,
wondering if efficient executive Kate had fallen off a cliff.

"I'll join you in a little over half an hour," she said, patting
his cheek with a tenderness that took both of them by surprise,
and walked swiftly away from him. She turned once and saw
him standing in the same spot, looking after her; looking,
strange for a man so big, so tall, strange for a sixty-five-
thousand-a-year vice-president, lost.

There was no hiding place as far as she could see from here,
even for a slight thin man, on the moors. She thought she might
try the beach below; for all she knew, sandpipers and gulls,
shells and seaweeds, might be part of his researches.

She remembered from childhood a way down the towering
face of the bluff, navigable if you kept your wits and your
muscles about you, and was reassured to find that at this age,
legs scissoring, body at a forty-five-degree angle, hands clutching at tufts of grass and beach plum branches, she could still
manage the descent, with only one brief unplanned slide.

The tide was in. Not a heavy surf but a misleading huge
lazy billow almost level with the sand. She had been caught
in that swelling high-tide billow once, the sand shelving down
precipitously, and taken deep and spun head over heels, not
knowing which was sea bottom and which was hidden air and
sky, or in what direction she was headed, Massachusetts or
Portugal. It was only blind luck, or God, that had made her
final despairing choice right, a summoning of strength that shot
her head out of the water and let her frantic feet find the climb
of the shelf and tumble her free on the sand.

It was the closest as far as her own memory went that she
had ever come to death. But what an unlikely word, idea,
death—here on this timeless beach, with the gently swinging
sea dark grape-blue, the lion-colored bluffs soaring to the sky,
the sand sending up crystals of light.

She was proved immediately wrong in this comfortable assumption. With a small grief, she stepped over the stiff smashed
body of a sea gull.

And then, her attention caught by a bird's whirring whistle—

surely not a pheasant, this close to the sea?—looked to her left, and saw in a position of a sleeper a pair of legs trousered in flannel, a tweed elbow, the rest concealed by a large bony portion of a tree trunk that appeared to be dried to the consistency of rock, knife-finned like a shark, at the foot of the sand cliff.

Sleepers on beaches were a commonplace, but the legs should be jeaned.

She didn't want to go and investigate the sleeper.

Something held her back, a lifelong habit of fleeing from crashes, thuds, sirens, disasters; walk hastily and look hastily the other way, from the people gathering to have a front seat at some interesting tragedy freshly soaked in blood.

But she saw in imagination a blue, blue gaze of disbelief and contempt.

"And you didn't stop to see if he was alive or dead? You didn't even look?"

She looked.

He looked, too, not at her, out of his greenish eyes, but at a branch of beach plum above his head, although the head itself was at a wrong angle.

There was no blood, but there was a sense of something irretrievably dropped, and broken, smashed.

Her eyes went up the murderous heights, leaning in toward the two of them, a little, here. Far above her head was a glint. A pair of glasses hanging from a tiny fir tree.

She made no sound but walked rapidly away, stepping again over the dead gull, up the beach, and suddenly, when her legs wouldn't hold her up any more, she sat down on a shapely piece of gray driftwood, studied for some moments a beer can on the sand, and then let her face fall into her palms.

Fingers, on her bent shoulders. A terrible shudder happened under his hand. Concerned arms lifted her up.

"Kate, what in God's name, what's the matter, did something frighten you?"

She stared at him in an uncomprehending manner.

"But how did you—?"

"I was worried about you. I followed you. At first with

these." He touched the binoculars. "And then on foot, I saw you stop, with Vin, did something happen with him to make you—"

"That man. Up there, not far. . . ." She gestured with an arm. "Past a dead sea gull, and then to the left, at the foot of the cliff, behind a shark-looking kind of huge chunk of old washed-up wood—oh, and I think he's dead."

She sounded to herself like some friendly soul directing a motorist to the correct turnoff for the destination he wanted.

She watched him running up the beach from her, again an illusive picture, splendid speech of a tall well-muscled body in a festive blaze of sun beside the morning sea.

He was back in a few minutes. "Yes. He is."

Curiously expressionless voice, face. Shock, probably. Which was what must be wrong with her, too, this feeling nothing, nothing at all, except how warm the sun was on her hair.

"I told you," scolding, "I didn't want us to split up," and then he drew a long breath and reached for her hand and pulled her to her feet. "Can you make it back up the way you came down? I'll be right behind you in case you slip."

"Yes, I think so." And conversationally, almost gaily, "It's easier going up than coming down, as a matter of fact."

He gave her face a close look and said harshly, "And for Christ's sake don't get the vapors or hysterics halfway up and topple back on me," and the hard slap in his voice summoned her back a little from her unnatural wandering.

Efficiently and speedily, she climbed, pulled herself up over the edge, wanted to lie on the grass but didn't. He was instantly behind her and beside her.

"Give me your hand." Not warmly, playfully, this time. A necessity, there were things to be done right away and she was a burden.

From a roadside telephone booth not far from where he had parked the Ford, he called the police, gave them his information in a few succinct sentences, and said yes, he would meet the police car at the North Truro crossroads and direct them to the body.

Kate continued to be a burden to him. Getting back into the car, he said, "I'll drive you to the house and drop you off, I have to go back there and show them where he is and how he was found, I found him, you didn't. Can you get lost, up in your room, reading or something, for a while?"

"Why? Yes, though—of course I can—"

"*Why?* It's time to turn your mind on, Kate. Not that it couldn't be—" He stared at the road ahead of him. This had been the day he was going to clear things up and shove them into their proper niches.

He stopped at the hedge opening. "Don't say anything at all to anybody, am I getting through to you? Nothing at all beyond a nice good morning."

"Yes, Jack," obediently, "all right."

He hesitated and then said, "I have a few minutes," and walked with her to the door and watched while she went up the stairs.

She had closed her door and was leaning against it when there was a light knock and his own name in a murmur. She opened it and his hand came in with a small glass of brandy, and then there was the sound of his feet on the stairs, a quiet unhurried descent.

FIFTEEN

"Just to be covered," Sergeant Coles explained almost apologetically to the *Times* man at his elbow, as they watched Sergeant Oro photographing Mr. Spiggott's body under the beach plum branches. "Routine, you know, while Doc's on the way, and to cover the outside chance that there might be any question at all. . . ."

Carefully making it clear that he was not a small-town cop playing at detecting.

"Poor fellow." He said it with genuine shocked regret, his kind eyes on the angled position of the head. "We've had to pull him out of trouble before, but never . . . Ran into a nest of wasps once, up Pilgrim Lake way, all but got stung to death. Another time got his foot caught in a trap in the woods. Accident-prone, they call it. He might've seen something just over the edge up there and reached for it. Or turned giddy and lost his balance, heights do funny things to people. And I don't think he sees all that well, you'd notice him squinting even with those heavy glasses on. . . ."

His listener felt himself overtaken by an astonished flooding sense of relief. Never mind, at the moment, the deep feeling of guilt.

He had been rehearsing mentally a list of mights and maybes.

You see, it's this way, Sergeant. Someone in my family might have killed my uncle.

Mr. Spiggott happened to be around at the time and might have heard or seen or picked up something that would, the more he thought about it, lead to some kind of identification.

There was nothing conclusive in the story he told my Uncle Leo—I heard it and someone else might have been listening too, there are two inside doors to the office, one very handily on the way to the upstairs bathroom.

But Leo's an impatient man and didn't want ramblings, reminiscences, bits and pieces, about that night, lawyers like things nice and clean, wrapped up, especially if they happen to be among the heirs.

And someone might have said some way or another, Come into my parlor, Mr. Spiggott, my parlor being the moors and the edge of the cliff, and either struck him a killing blow on the skull and shoved him over, or took his chances with one hard push.

Although the signs of a heavy blow would after all be consistent with a fast, bouncing final fall—there are rocks protruding halfway down, and that great shark of wood at the bottom.

Hail and farewell, Mr. Spiggott. I have enough trouble on my hands without you, considering the Grahn woman . . . but she can't very well be killed because too many people heard what she said. Including an independent witness with nothing to gain or lose, that little pug-faced ex-secretary. Or just at the moment, I don't *think* she can be killed. . . .

And now he wasn't going to have to say a damned thing, raise any questions at all, because Sergeant Coles was patiently explaining Mr. Spiggott's accidental death to him.

He looked away from the body. The sense of guilt made him say abruptly, "My uncle may have been the last person to see him alive, back at the house. I don't know—perhaps you'd like to have a talk with him."

"Well, of course the poor fellow would have come around to pay his respects, he spoke highly of Mr. Converse. I don't think there's any need to bother your uncle, particularly at a time like this." The sergeant gave an appropriate sigh.

"There's no question of suicide in my mind, he enjoyed life, you know, his weeds and all, happy as a clam roaming around. And to my knowledge he hadn't an enemy in the world, people liked him, everybody knew him. Sad business. Sad.''

All taken care of, then; nothing for anyone to worry about.

But if there was a person with a certain worry, he didn't know yet, couldn't know, that as far as the police were concerned he was free and clear of the murder of Mr. Thomas Spiggott.

There was a light knock at the bedroom door.

Turn your mind on, Kate, don't say anything to anybody beyond a nice good morning.

She opened the door to Sophie, who gave her a long look and said, ''Mercy's sake, Kate, you seein' ghosts, what's the matter?'' Her eyes went beyond Kate to the half-full brandy glass on the windowsill, where Kate had been standing, watching for Jack to come back.

''Bad night,'' Kate said.

''I hope,'' Sophie said, ''my radio didn't keep you awake. I fell asleep with it on but then I was wakeful, too, and there was an awful lot of comin' and goin', wasn't there, maybe Marcia tottin' up valuables and that trashy Tike thievin' again, and I swear and declare I heard the First Prize's manly tones at some ungodly hour. . . . As that brandy's goin' idle, I'll have a sip if you don't mind.''

She took more than a sip. Her long shapely hand was steady. ''Speakin' of the First Prize, have you any idea where his researches took him this mornin'? I only ask because he seems to be givin' you marked and particular looks from time to time, I thought you might be in on what he's up to—''

It was grotesque to feel even for a moment that she had to be careful with Sophie.

Kind, talented, dashingly successful Sophie.

But it suddenly occurred to her that in a real sense she didn't know Sophie very well, hadn't known her for very long—two or three years—and knew only family things about her childhood and her youth, the things you overheard, telephone conversations, dinner table talk, relatives chattering.

Her father, Anthony Converse, had left her mother when

Sophie was two years old; nobody knew exactly why. Although an educated guess was reasonable, a burnt-out love affair between people who had nothing, really, to say to each other except with their bodies.

From remote depths of memory, Kate summed up her Aunt Marcia saying, "A village girl, I believe, some steaming swamp, and he was down there staying with the *Montmorencys* when he met her and three days later they were married. . . ."

Nobody had heard from Anthony Converse for thirty-six years. If Sophie had, she hadn't passed along the information. He was, in the family mind, dead and buried somewhere, an adventurous reckless handsome man who would have nothing to do with a profession, an office; he had loved horses and was buying and selling and training them when he went to Mississippi and met Sophie's mother, Lindy Lacey.

To everybody's astonishment, Lindy Lacey Converse would have no part of the family, no help, no money; she did not take to spurning. She went to work, where, Kate couldn't remember, a factory, a drugstore? Sophie had had a hard rough time as a child and young girl; they had been chitlins and collard greens poor, she once, lightly, said to Kate.

Sophie, in high school, had gotten a scholarship to an, as described by her, "ass-in-pockets nowhere art school in Atlanta," and had studied costume design and fashion illustration.

And had made her long climb the tough and old-fashioned and difficult way, ambition, enormously hard work, on the outskirts of fashion drawing, merchandising, Atlanta, then Richmond, then Philadelphia, then New York, at last getting into a good Seventh Avenue house, Bland and Bahr, Juniors, paying her way as she was apprenticing as a designer by modeling and fighting off the hands in the dressing room, Mr. Bahr saying, Let's see, what exact size bust, hips, rear, my dear?

By taking great risks and throwing herself passionately into the fray, she had become Sophie Converse, Inc., and got her own banks of windows in lustrous stores, as Halston and Blass and Saint Laurent did. To appear in a Converse in some circles was a good deal better than to display your first mink.

She was wearing one of her own dresses now, throwaway

elegant, ivory on white wool gingham, long willowy top over a circle of skirt that began at the hips, long graceful legs, bronze kid tap-dancing pumps bow-tied with grosgrain ribbon.

To fill the small silence in which some sort of lie might be framed—and Sophie's known biography, browsed through, had taken Kate only about four seconds in the illimitable computer of the human mind—Kate said, ''Jack? I suppose he's restless, cooped up here. . . . You look marvelous, Sophie. How much does that one cost?''

''Nine hundred dollars,'' Sophie said. ''To get back to the dear inquirin' boy—I saw you goin' off in the car together earlyish, that makes two restless people by my count. I went down and with my own fair hands and under Mrs. Groin's eldritch glare made him my flannel cakes that he loves, they'll toughen up if they sit at the back of the stove over hot water much longer.'' Absent-mindedly, she finished the brandy. ''With dark deeds in the air, I might point out you're no good at connivin'.''

''Sophie, I honestly have no idea when he'll be back to eat your flannel cakes.'' Nice to find something to say that was the exact truth.

''When who'll be back?'' a voice asked from the stairwell.

Kate went to the open door and looked down at a girl standing tentatively at halfway point, a lovely moony girl with ashen blue eyes, hair so pale a blond as to seem silvery in this light, a charmingly beaked fine nose.

''I'm sorry to invade you, but the front door was open and I heard Sophie's voice up above. . . .''

Kate recognized her after a second or two. On the television screen, interviewing Mike Mansfield or Charles Percy or Hubert Humphrey, her close-up on camera at the end of the news segment, ''This is Eugenia Pell''—Somebody's news, she couldn't remember which network—''on Capitol Hill.''

Behind her, Sophie said, ''Your quarry's temporarily unavailable, Eugenia, out somewhere, I want him too, what hies you so far from the Potomac?''

''I started early on a weekend in Hyannisport and I thought it would be only decent to—'' She hesitated. ''I only met Jack's uncle once but we liked each other. But as long as *he's* not here, will you tell him I'll stop back later? Just for a minute, of course," and she ran down the stairs and out the door.

"Nothin' like checkin' your chickens to see the foxes haven't got at them," Sophie said. "Poor policy, though, with him. Showin' your hand and stakin' your claim. It's my belief she's for fun and not to marry, as far as he's concerned. Not as ghastly as Tike, there's ladylike icin' on this one's cake, but still, another get-out-of-my-way girl."

"Attractive, though, very," Kate said, deeply thoughtful and strangely pierced. What was this sudden hot and cold, uncomfortable feeling, a light somewhere dimmed and blinking out?

And then she remembered why she was in semi-hiding, and made an abrupt return to real things, terrible things, like Mr. Spiggott.

Unsummoned, a picture of Vin sprang into her mind, begging her, on the moors, to come back to the house with him. "Please, Kate, please . . ."

Please don't go and look over the edge of the cliff, Kate?

"We're due at our battle stations," Sophie said. "There's a mighty lot of mournin' down there already."

She couldn't, without making an odd point of it, hang back in her room from her family duty of receiving condolences from strangers.

The living room was full again, but as it was morning, and too early for all but the bravest souls to approach the buffet of drinks, the atmosphere, while at a mild boil of interest, conversation, was not a party one.

"You'd never know," a sour teetotal female voice said to someone, behind her, "he drank whiskey every day, even for *lunch*. He looks quite healthy, I'll say that for him."

"I heard"—another voice, the speaker invisible beyond two large tall white-haired men who looked like bankers—"that there was something funny, about his death, I mean—" and then the voice stopped as one of the bankers, in mid-sentence about the German mark, turned and stared.

There was a tickle of ice along Kate's spine. After a barely noticeable pause, she retrieved her own sentence, left hanging: "Yes, I'm sure Mrs. Grahn will see that his library books are returned."

The tall lean woman she was talking to said hastily, "I'm not worried about the books, I just wanted to make the point that he's, he was, a great reader, and a fast one, often five books at a time and then he'd be back after just a few days, for more, we'll miss him—"

It was odd that you could carry on an almost rational conversation with someone and yet beam your ears, simultaneously recording other people's words; this worked particularly well if you were very attracted to someone at a middle distance from you, or were very worried about something.

The look of intense anxiety on Marcia's face, turned to Glenna's—what was that about?

"As the eldest member of the family and, to put it mildly, the least prosperous, except perhaps for Timothy, surely there will be no question that the table will go to me. And he'd only smear it with paint and burn it with his cigarettes."

Where was Jack? Would he be accompanied by towering policemen raising a thunder of knocking at the front door?

Empty the room. This is an order. The Converse family is under arrest.

Unreal, all of it, facial muscles beginning to ache with polite smiles, the scent of white lilacs from a few feet away making her feel a little ill—she hoped white lilacs wouldn't be spoiled for her forever, she loved them—Mrs. Grahn going about collecting coffee cups and looking explosive again, eyes red, plump lips pursed; a sudden storm of sneezing from Vin, and Glenna saying, "It's those asters, you're allergic to them, remember? Go out and get some air."

Jule Remond, going by, gave her a sympathetic light tap on her forearm as she made her way to the coffin. Jule wasn't of this atmosphere at all; Kate connected her with summer nights, over the bay, great platters of red lobsters, candles flickering, "Another round of drinks? At once, mon cher Mr. Converse, and"—snapping her fingers at a passing peasant-clothed young waitress—"more drawn butter here, more lemon, and a fresh loaf of bread."

As she was giving to a plump little woman her permission to remove some bulbs from Phip's garden—"his *Iris kaempferi*, he was so proud of it, the blossoms almost a foot across, you know, white, I'd like to think of it as a sort of living memorial to him, and I'd take such care of them"—she saw Jule rise from the kneeler and, with a gesture that reminded her of Jack, brush the tears from her face.

Sophie was nearby. Jule stopped in front of her and said, "Eleven o'clock or not, I would like to toast him, will you join me in a little, a very little, champagne?"

"Gladly," Sophie said.

". . . and the rose-red ones, too, beautifully mottled, do you think anyone would mind?" Not at all, Kate assured the plump woman.

As Jule, so thin and small, Sophie, so gracefully dominating in size, picked their way through bodies, she heard Jule say, "For a while there, I thought you weren't speaking to me—last Sunday, remember, when I passed you going the other way at Dutra's Corners, you heading out, I figured, to Mr. Converse's but," charitably, "it was late in the day and raining, so I guess you didn't see me even though I tooted at you three times."

Rose-red and mottled, Kate thought; that was what had happened to Sophie's face, and it took a few seconds for the cause of the color to register with her.

Last Sunday?

It would have been the most natural thing in the world for Sophie to have said, My God, and I was only up there Sunday, to think that two days later he . . .

But she hadn't said it to Kate and obviously not to anyone, for if she had, it would have been one of those openly mused upon coincidences, events, that formed part of the vivid history of any death in a family.

Yes, think of it, Sophie, being there just two days before he died, voices would marvel, recollect. *Having no idea, no idea at all. . . .*

Sophie passed on her way to champagne about three feet from her, looking neither to the left nor to the right but steadily ahead, as if by sheer will denying the possibility of family ears able to listen, family eyes examining.

Kate knew the ostrich feeling and had on occasion practiced it herself: if you don't, deliberately, see or hear them, there's really no one there to see or hear you. One only adopted this assumption in a sudden surge of humiliation or panic.

She felt Jack's entrance into the room before she saw him, and Sophie was swept instantly from her mind. He made his way as directly as was possible to her and examined her face silently and minutely.

"I had to come down and help. This mob . . ." and waited for him to administer a shared and awful blow.

Or a second one, this morning.

"For the moment, if you can believe it," his voice close to her ear, his lips scarcely moving, "everything is all right."

They looked in complicity at each other; there might have been nobody else there, for a flash of time, nobody but the two of them.

The long attractive dents on either side of his mouth deepened with tension. The casual eye might have recorded it as a smile.

She felt and then knew in that peculiar island they were on that he wanted badly to touch her, reassure her, comfort her and perhaps himself.

He added, his eyes a burn of blue, "All right, for the living, that is."

SIXTEEN

He thought it might be an idiotic idea, but it seemed to him almost a necessity of conscience.

Timothy and Tike weren't visible, but on the whole the Converses were well represented.

The worst they could say was, Poor Jack, up to his ass in scotch, he kept buttonholing everybody and blurting out these ridiculous announcements.

Poor Jack, he remembered, halfway across the room. "Newspaperman found dead at foot of Atlantic bluffs. Police concluded that John Converse in his grief . . ."

Except that it was not his body, but Thomas Spiggott's.

He had already cautioned Kate to stay, conversationally speaking, out of trouble. "Go over there and talk to Mrs. Lanzo, that fat woman. You couldn't be safer in church, she's the town's champion bore and avoided like the plague."

He went into the dining room, first, and ducked to drop a kiss on Jule's forehead.

To Sophie he said abruptly and softly, "They've found him."

Sophie's face was looking blanched, taut. After a second or so, she said, "Found who? An honest man, finally? Some local Diogenes had some luck with his lantern?"

The words sounded like Sophie, but the voice didn't sound right at all.

He snatched an answer from the air. "Father McAloon. He was supposed to be here but he stopped off—" and disliking

119

the taste of suspicion, betrayal, on his lips, turned and moved away.

"For a moment," Jule said, after a thoughtful sip of champagne, "I thought Jacques meant Mr. Spiggott."

"Why? Has someone gone and mislaid the man Spiggott? Well, anyway, cheers, Jule," lifting her glass.

Leo loomed by the bookshelves, surveying the room with a look of severe depression.

"They've—the police—found him," Jack said.

Leo gave him his considering, lawyer's look and didn't respond immediately. Then he rumbled, "Good. Although I'm inclined to question the use of police in what might be termed purely social circumstances. He was one of Phip's oldest friends and he'd kick himself if he didn't get here in time."

"Who?"

"What the hell is this, Alice in Wonderland? I've had my secretary in New York telephoning all over the state of Maine trying to find MacPartland, he's on a hunting trip up there and I thought—"

"Well, that's good, then, isn't it."

"I hope," Leo said as his nephew started a quick purposeful swivel, "you don't go about your daily work in this disconnected way. You sound like a misprint, or several. Not usual for the *Times*."

Marcia's reaction was a look of great fatigue, a small sharp shake of her head as if to clear it, make it work, and she said, "I'm so horribly tired, I can't seem to follow—who? I mean, who are they and who is *him*?"

"Father McAloon."

"Ohhh. . . ." A long sigh, and then a squaring of the shoulders. "But in any case I assume he'll be around for the rosary this evening."

He was tempted to drop it. His family was a highly intelligent crew, and whoever it was, if it had been anyone—if Sergeant Coles wasn't after all perfectly correct in his conclusions—would be braced now, prepared, knowing that sooner or later a surf caster or a beach buggy or a seaside stroller would come upon the body of Mr. Spiggott.

But he remembered his own binocular view, a Kate, a Vin, close, readable, her gentle touch on Vin's cheek. Assisted or unassisted eyes might have secretly watched Kate crouching numbed at the side of a body under a beach plum.

And he wanted badly the blank stare of comfortable innocence, not the terror of the trapped and almost caught, or the brainy nimble concealment of it.

Vin was standing beside Glenna near the coffin. At Jack's murmured information, Glenna went an alarming white and Vin's arm shot out to hold her upright.

"Nice time, nice place, for whatever bomb you think you're dropping; causing someone to faint into the coffin isn't my idea of polite wake behavior—" His eyes blazed.

Glenna seemed to be having trouble getting words out. "Vinnie?" Shakily she forced out her son's name. "When we last heard, he was in Florida, but you make him sound . . . dead or something. . . ."

"He's dead, but it isn't Vinnie," Jack said, his eyes not on her face but on Vin's. "Man by the name of Spiggott. You remember, in the doorway last night."

"Well, as your police chief friend says, it happens," Vin said. "As illustrated directly behind me."

If there had been any kind of thin ice for him, he had crossed it safely; he was in hard command of himself. "Excuse me while I put my wife back together again with a drink. Come on, Glen . . . you'll be all right. . . ."

Garrett was standing near a tubbed palm tree as tall as he was. He was holding a sort of informal court, or one-man receiving line.

"Senator, such an honor to . . ."

"But you look just the way you do on television!"

"Garrett, boy." One of the bankers, money speaking to power, well understanding each other.

Jack eased himself into the line and with a sardonic smile extended a hand and said, "Greetings, Senator, as this seems to be the order of the day. . . . Well, they found him."

Garrett had come into a brief bloom under the tendered respects, the open American bow to titles. His hair glowed white, his skin pink, his eyes a candid light-filled blue; a sort of makeup of esteem covering the gray, the shadows, the flickering watchful lines.

His grip of Jack's hand, in his own large one, became a crunch, as though he would like to break the strong bones.

"Hello there, Judas," his voice very soft.

Jack glanced over at Kate by chance or on purpose, and saw a sudden flinching look on her face. She couldn't, at that distance, and listening to Mrs. Lanzo about her seashell collecting, have heard what Garrett said?

"Found him?—them?—her?" Garrett said in the same soft voice. "I think I may know what you're talking about but you're not making yourself very clear. Funny, I thought it would be all quiet on the western front until my brother was decently underground."

One hand in his pocket; jingling sounds.

"But not right here, right now, do you mind? Before all these people, I don't like to count out your coins."

SEVENTEEN

". . . And one lucky day, in the rain, I came upon an Atlantic shark eye snail, no resemblance to your northern moon snail, quite a glamorous shell, ivory, or cream, with a sort of purplish-colored eye. . . ."

Kate felt she had been under this particular shellfire long enough; at least nine or ten minutes of it, and besides, she thought that in some way, without a word or a gesture, she had been signaled.

"Excuse me, I must go help in the kitchen for a bit," she said mendaciously, and drifted through the busy room, turned at a tall lighted coffin candle, and pushed open the kitchen door, very much aware of someone almost immediately on her heels. Surely not Mrs. Lanzo with still another shell?

Mrs. Grahn was standing talking into the wall phone next to the door, completing a grocery order in a manner that somehow combined normal and dreadful: ". . . a dozen juice oranges, one of them was rotten last delivery, I'll thank you for an extra one free, two quarts of milk, a roll of paper towels, two pounds of Canadian bacon, and that's all, and the final bill, just to remind you, this will be Mr. Converse's last order."

Kate felt a propelling hand at the small of her back and found herself in the large airy pantry to the right of the black iron stove. The pantry door was quietly closed behind the two of them.

She had forgotten what pleasant places old-fashioned pantries

were. This one had a large window at the far end, with a long
distended white muslin bag, or stomach, of cooked beach plums
hanging by a white string from the sash latch. Fragrant dark
red juice dripped gently into a large yellow crockery bowl.
Wasps buzzed in frustration just outside the screen. The long
neat shelves on either side, going up to the ceiling, were laden
with food with expensive names, Peek Freans, Fortnum and
Mason, S. S. Pierce, Fauchon.

Funny, jelly in the making, as though life in the house was
to go on serenely; as though the curtain hadn't come down on
it. But she supposed that Mrs. Grahn wouldn't want a basket
of picked beach plums to go to waste.

"Nice in here, isn't it," Jack said.

She turned and looked up into his face. "You're a little
. . . bruised, aren't you. He called you Judas."

"Yes, but he got it a bit wrong, if he's Christ, he wouldn't
be counting out the coins for me, it was the opposition party
that paid up."

"Well, after him, after that, after this morning, I'm on your
side. I don't pass, any more, and really didn't back then, but
I was worried about other people—"

"You are? Really? It's nice to have you on my side, Kate."

Hands beginning lightly at her shoulders and moving as
lightly down, he took her carefully into his arms, and moved
her closer to him, and then very close.

She understood. *Judas* . . . How alone he must feel.

But then, his face angled in against her throat, a warm-cool
feeling of fine firm thoughtful lips moving on the long tendon
just behind her ear, the mouth browsing, resting.

"Jack—"

"Just for a moment. Stay still." His voice came through her
flesh and blood, not her ears. She felt rather than heard his
long sigh—pleasure, regret? Some kind of sad sweet might-
have-been?—and then with the impact on her of a pistol shot at
close range he gave an inarticulate sharp cry and the peaceful
sunny pantry seemed to explode as he backed away from her.

He clapped his hand to the back of his neck. He saw her
stunned face and burst out laughing.

"I'm sorry, Kate, a hornet just stung me, a goddamned interfering hornet."

From about six feet outside the pantry window a voice said over a caught-back choke of laughter, "That could be none other than Jack Converse. I'm on my way to the front door."

"I forgot to tell you," Kate said, voice calm. She didn't know how she managed it over the pounding of her heart, shaking her inwardly like a tree in a windstorm, although nothing showed. "Your girl, Eugenia, came by and said she'd be back. I'll just, if you like, put a little bicarbonate of soda paste on the sting, and then you can—"

He looked startled and for a moment enraged: the sting or Eugenia?

"I wish you would," he said. "It hurts like hell. As though someone lit a match and is still holding it there flaming away. The bastard—" His eye caught the hornet, hovering about the overhead light bulb; he reached up two hands and smacked them disposingly together.

"Nice catch, but you could have been stung again," she said severely.

"That's how much you know about it, he contributed his stinger to me, but considering his timing he was asking for extinction anyway."

She spotted the yellow box of soda, mysteriously placed beside the jar of Madras curry powder. No, not a mystery, she thought, the large jar to guide Mrs. Grahn's hand logically when indigestion struck.

Businesslike, swift, she went out into the kitchen and made a spoonful of the paste. "Bend your head down."

"Your hands are shaking."

"You scared the hell out of me."

"But not away from my side? You're still on it, I hope?"

Mrs. Grahn was watching the medical attentions with a cold inquiring eye. Kate couldn't say, in front of her, that she was of course still on his side, as far as family alliances went, as far as his stare at truth, however disastrous, went; that far and no further.

"Are there Band-Aids anywhere, Mrs. Grahn? Otherwise

this paste will dry and fall off, your shirt collar barely misses it.''

Mrs. Grahn expressionlessly supplied the box of bandages.

The back of his neck was delightful. Shamelessly fair, smooth-skinned for a man. Strong and shapely, the muscles stirring lightly and responsively under her fingers.

''Trembling or not, you're very good at taking care of the grievously wounded, Kate.''

Mrs. Grahn had turned away. He took her right hand and put a quick kiss into her palm. ''Thank you.''

''Hadn't you better go out to your—to the Capitol Hill girl? I don't think she knows anyone here but Sophie.''

''—And handling my social life so nicely too, above and beyond the call of duty.''

The faintly bruised look around his eyes had disappeared. He looked for a moment vividly happy. Of course. That moony girl out there, waiting for him.

''Mr. Converse,'' Mrs. Grahn said in formal tones, ''I am going now to the town dump. I have no more room for my trash,'' gesturing at the slant-lidded wooden container built against the back of the house.

As this seemed to call for some kind of response. ''Very good,'' he said, and added, ''You have a great deal to do, with this crowd here,'' and was repelled at this false shadow-groping politeness on his own part.

''Yes. A very great deal to do.'' The back door closed behind her.

''I don't think I'd have done very well in the Balkans,'' Jack said to Kate. ''Things tend to stick in my craw. . . . But anyway, nurse, the Spiggott report. The police tell me firmly it's an accident.''

''An accident.'' Quiet voice. ''Oh.''

''And that's your belief, hell or high water. I did some slithering around in the grass, in there, because they'd have no way of knowing yet what the official conclusion was. My findings are zero, except that Glenna thought I had heard her son was dead and almost fainted. God, if only Mrs. Grahn would deposit herself in the town dump. For good.''

An accident. Cling to it for a while, in spite of what he was telling her between his lines. An accident.

• • •

There was a spill-out of people on the front lawn. The warm sunlight flared on the edge of crystal glasses and caught radiant trails of cigarette smoke. Shoulders were clapped, hands shaken, as old friend was briefly reunited with old friend, courtesy of Phip. Marcia, who had not ceased to deplore the festive air of the proceedings, was herself surrounded by elderly ladies with elegantly blued hair, murmuring to each other and sipping sherry; they looked as if they had come for bridge.

Eugenia was talking to Glenna, who she had once met at a party, near the catalpa tree when simultaneously with Jack's joining them Garrett emerged from the front door.

His eyes went instantly to Eugenia, tall and silvery in the sun, and the color left his face. Either with shock or clumsiness, he seemed to be on the point of stumbling off the high single brick step. A man's hand went out to steady him.

"Hi, Senator," Eugenia called gaily.

He walked to her and said harshly, making no attempt to lower his voice, the question seeming to be snatched out of him, "Do we assume a camera crew a mile or so behind you?"

Eugenia looked over the broad threatening shoulder.

"Jack, help," she said. She walked around Garrett and kissed Jack on the edge of his jaw. Kate, four feet away, observed the casual possessiveness of the light kiss before strangers.

"Eugenia is not here professionally," Jack said.

"Oh? Yet *another* in your gallery of girls?" Still angry, taken off balance, striking out, his lips just faintly shaking.

"Yes, yet another," Eugenia said in a sweet stung voice. She raised her glass. "Here's to you and your Banking Reform Committee. And while we're at it, let's drink to numbered Bahamian bank accounts."

"For Christ's sake, Eugenia—" Jack looked in alarm at Garrett's face and stance of absolute drained stillness.

"Well, as they say, hell hath no fury. So far it's only a rumor, Senator Converse. That I picked up in the gallery. On the Hill, that is."

EIGHTEEN

"Where," Timothy asked Tike casually, "does our progenitor lay his head at night?"

"Why? Did you want to arrange an interview in private? More secrets? He's available right now, if you want him. Something's wrong with Garrett and Daddy's trying to cure it with brandy."

"All right for you, Tike. I haven't, by the way, told anyone about your kissing a corpse for a camera. Yet."

"Some people called the Wymans, Wyman's Lane, Truro, the name's on the mailbox. They're abroad. He's known them for years. I met the son somewhere, I can't remember his name now but"—she flicked the tip of her tongue over the corner of her upper lip—"he was loads of fun."

She drifted into the living room and for a while amused herself by being looked at; looked at with particular fervor by men she classified as old, forty or over. It hadn't yet palled, using other people's faces as mirrors giving back heady reflections of herself.

She had shed her secondhand clothes and her siren's satin for a long dress of gray dimity tiny-flowered in dim blue and brown, caught in with brown velvet ribbon under her breasts; a mournful but enchanting costume.

"You poor child," a dark bearded man said, finding her pensively studying a newly arrived floral offering as tall as she was, branches of rhododendron embroidered and garlanded

128

with pale pink roses and sunk in waist-high fountains of fern. (That's not a bouquet, Tike thought, that's a whole goddamn *glen*.)

The man went on consolingly, patting her shoulder, "He had a good life, a long life. It mustn't seem real to you at all, though, death."

Tike without any effort at all managed one tear for each eye. She made no attempt to wipe away the two pearls of water slipping down the tight silk of her cheeks.

Looking, with a long responding sigh, past the bearded man, she saw Timothy getting into her green MG. The nerve of it—she always forgot to take out the ignition key, but anyway, this place was supposed to be safe, there was even a traffic cop to help out with any parking problems or intrusive carloads of curious people attracted here by the newspaper stories about Phip.

She gave Timothy a minute or two and then floated through the front door and looked in a shopping kind of way up and down the line of cars parked on both sides of the road.

In Vin's present shape, he was probably as bad about his ignition key as she was. Correct. She climbed into his black Cadillac and started the engine.

The Wymans' house, half hidden up a shadowy lane, was a sprawl of gray fieldstone, shuttered and awninged in pale blue, deep in a grove of spruce and hemlock. She stopped the car just short of a curve that hid the house and went quickly through the trees and, staying close against the house, to the front door. He had left it unlocked.

She was wearing soft ballet practice slippers that made no sound as she crossed the wide hall and listened at the foot of the stairway. Footsteps, above and to the right, not exactly tiptoeing, but careful.

The house was cold and smelled sweetly of recent wood fires. Holding her long skirt in one hand, she ran up the carpeted stairs and paused when she neared a door that was six or seven inches open. She passed the opening and applied an eye to the hinged crack on the other side.

Timothy was busily, neatly searching. She almost giggled. He looked so silly in that rumpled cream suit, with somebody's gloves on, heavy yellow pigskin, certainly not his, they were expensive.

He went patiently through a long wall of shelves and closets. The built-in unit stopped about a foot short of the high ceiling and had a decorative molding on top in a Greek key design. He reached up an arm and put a hand over and beyond the molding and began patting his way along the length of it. With a small pleased sound, he took down a large flat oblong object wrapped in heavy brown paper.

He was quietly and carefully removing the wrapping when Tike's voice, apparently from nowhere, and unidentifiable, whispered, ''What the hell do you think you're doing?''

He went a scary dirty gray color under his bronze, stood perfectly still for a few seconds, and then with a squaring of his shoulders walked rapidly to the door and yanked it open and gazed pinpointed at his sister.

''Glad to see your nerve is up to par,'' she said. ''That was real brave of you, Timo.'' Slipping past him, ''I want to see what it is that you're stealing.''

She ripped the brown paper off and stood looking at the watercolor. ''Oh—just that old sailboat thing.''

He reached for it and snatched it away from her and through the torn paper at the back she saw the melting cream and rose and gold, and one shadowy blue eye and moonlit pale fingers busy at the end of a plait. She leaned forward and tore off the rest of the paper and saw the signature. Degas.

Virtuously indignant, she said, ''This must be worth a fortune!''

''Okay, Tike,'' he said. ''You go to your church and I'll go to mine,'' which between them meant, You leave me alone and I'll leave you alone. ''I wanted to salvage something. In case everything goes down the drain. This'll keep me off the streets for a while, researching for Forbes. 'Madam, which of these silver patterns do you like best? Please grade your choices by number, best liked to least liked. Or, would you mind telling me what your husband eats for breakfast? Will you have him try out this cereal and fill out this questionnaire?'—For God's sake shut your mouth about it, will you?''

''But you can't sell a stolen painting—''

"You can sell anything if you go to the right people. You don't get the best price, but it's cash in hand."

In a delayed reaction, Tike said, "What do you mean, in case everything goes down the drain?"

"Well, you heard them talking—the old man too—about that dirty word 'litigation.' As Sophie said, Who killed Cock Robin, if anybody did, at all. Everybody's going to run around screaming, pointing the finger at each other, get somebody, nail him, it wasn't me, it was you, and before you know it, it will all be out in the open, the Converses' Watergate, somebody will blow the whistle, newspapers full of it, probate held up, sorry, no money until we get this cleared up, if we ever do, and time drags on and life goes by—" His eyes were savage.

"You don't need a crystal ball," Tike said. "If anybody did anything to anybody, it was Vin, of course, anybody can see that. And I guess, screw everything, I can see what you mean."

"—To say nothing of that redheaded bitch," Timothy said. "She may have another grenade in her back pocket, waiting for the best time to pull the pin out. Don't kid yourself that it's going to end when they say amen over Phip."

Tike stared at him. "But it's not *fair*—"

"Fair? What do you think people, all right people, do in their daily lives and look away from and say, Doesn't everybody? And *this*. Everybody has had this carrot under their nose for as long as I can remember, everything's going to be dandy eventually, Phip can't live forever. And then someone hears that maybe that woman was going to get to eat the carrot after all—"

"I don't mean fair that way. I mean, Vin shouldn't be able to get away with it, ruining people's lives. . . ."

Her speculative eyes met her brother's. "I mean, there must be a way, some way to *make* him—"

Timothy grinned. "You see what I mean about what some people will do? You'd build some kind of a trap and try to get that poor bastard to spring it on himself."

Tike's face closed. "Anyway, soul, you'd better get out of here with your painting and put it away safe and sound somewhere. Aren't you afraid Daddy might think it was you? And where did you get his keys, by the way, in case sometime I might need them?''

"Keys in his raincoat pocket. On a hook in the kitchen. And the other thing, can you see the respected lawyer hauling his only son into court on a charge of theft? And son says, to borrow from you—I heard about the spoons—Uncle Phip said he wanted me to have it. Or, worse, Well, my daddy's brother was murdered, and I thought what with the investigation it might be like forever before I'd see a penny of my money—''

Moved by a gust of October wind, a tree branch rocked and groaned outside the window. They both jumped.

"I said, let's go," Tike said warily. "You're some conspirator, some thief, running around in a collector's item car stealing artwork with"—she choked on a high laugh—"gloves on yet. I'll take the MG, you can stash the painting in Vin's car, help yourself." She hospitably waved the Cadillac keys. "And then you can take your time about where to hide it. If I didn't know you better, I'd think you were putting on some kind of ghastly high school play to make people think you have no idea what you're doing, just a dreamy, like, impractical artist.''

"Good idea, Vin's car, I never thought of it. In the trunk. The last thing anybody would connect him with is any kind of painting.''

Timothy, as they ran down the stairs together, turned his black sparkling eyes on her and added, "If I didn't know you better, I'd hate to have you on my tail for any reason. Except I don't, I suppose, know you any more. But in your dumb way—'artwork'! Jesus, *Degas*—you are sort of crazy bright, Tike.''

He had given the artist's name the educated final *s*.

"If you can't even pronounce it, I don't see how you can sell it," Tike said scathingly.

"By the way, why were you chasing me, spying on me?''

"I didn't like you taking off in my car that way. And besides, I was tired of looking at that old body lying there.''

NINETEEN

"It is frightful," Marcia said, "to have to discuss matters of the utmost importance while looking as if we were talking about what the weather will be like for the funeral."

"I'll help," Leo said, and tapped the glass of the barometer on the wall behind him. "Not a good outlook, not a good outlook at all."

"Must you sound that way, like doom?" She hoped instantly that nobody had heard her.

There was an alderman-looking person not four feet from her with a watch chain festooned across his pendulous stomach. He had, unnervingly to her, blessed himself at least three times while praying at Phip's coffin. Why?

Had he heard awful things and was he blessing away demons, bad deeds? Or perhaps placing his piety in a show window. . . .

But the subject had to be tackled.

"I wonder, Leo, as Phip's lawyer, if you should ask all these . . . people where they were on Tuesday night? Just in case the question might come up?"

Leo cast an eye at the watch-chained man and moved, turning his back to him.

"By all these people, you mean your, our, family?"

"Yes . . . with a view to possible future trouble. That terrible woman may be holding something back, waiting to make some pronouncement for television, I must say that Pell girl shows no kind of delicacy turning up here—"

"Might you be a bit rash, consulting me?" Leo asked with his dour grin. "If you really think there's something to this fantastic tale, you may recall that my own daughter listed me as a prime suspect. Where, by the way, were you that night?"

"At home, as I usually am, alone, reading."

"That building you live in, good address, but old, a perfect warren of entrances and exits . . . too bad you didn't have company."

"Leo."

"You see what I mean, though. Innocently at home but no way to prove it. And then, people in bed with other people, legally sanctioned or otherwise—anyone with half a brain can dig up someone to cover for him. And where was I, you ask? I too was alone, reading. The *Collected Poems* of W. B. Yeats, if I remember correctly. But unfortunately I haven't a doorman." Leo occupied his own brownstone on East Seventy-fourth Street.

Marcia was very pale. "Do you mean to say that this thing will haunt and threaten and pursue us forever? Not that," bitterly, "I have a great deal of forever left."

"An interesting line to take," Leo mused, "if *you*—sorry, I'm not serious. I tend to look at things in the abstract but we're all real, flesh and blood, aren't we. . . . Yes, Marcia, I do think it may be a permanent kind of question. Unless someone's conscience, or nerves, or alcohol gets the better of him—her—and our villain cracks conveniently wide open."

"But it's not to be endured, it can't be lived with—"

"I know you're a woman of certainties. In our day, everything was black and white, in a quite different sense of those words. But remember, we would not be the first family with a festering sore, as they say—a secret—covered up by mutual consent. All for one and one for all. Oh God, the phone again. . . ."

"For you, Jack," Sophie said. "For some strange reason, I seem to smell the press—I connect that dulcet Louisiana voice with public broadcastin', out of Washington, D.C."

Allender, a shy, soft-spoken, amiable man, said, "At a time like this . . . I don't like to . . . but we're getting odd sounds from Provincetown. Someone named Captiva who works for the local paper has sent us what he labels 'Special to the New York *Times*.' Very badly written, he seems not to have attended school. The gist being that there are stories going around the town that your uncle met with some kind of foul play because he was on the brink of—wait, I'll read it to you—'an autumn wedding with his glamorous titian-haired housekeeper, Mrs. Stella Grahn.' I suppose there's nothing in it?''

''I suppose there's nothing in it at all but libel. Does he have any suggestions about who's at the other end of the foul play?''

''No, only makes rough guesses about how much each member of the family stands to inherit, and goes on at length about the Converse collection, stolen whole from *Art News*, I remember reading the piece.''

''I'd better have a word with him, thanks for letting me know,'' Jack said, knowing that that had not quite been Allender's purpose for the call, and that Allender knew he knew it.

''Senator on the scene?''

''Yes.''

''Well, then,'' suddenly sounding embarrassed, ''good-by, and of course if there *is*—''

''Yes. Naturally. Of course.''

And then, in a manner not usual with him, he went on chattily, ''How's Myra? And the boys?'' Let Allender think he was for the moment soft-headed with grief.

It worked; he heard the careful click of a receiver being replaced. Either in this house, or in any room across the street.

Kate took a sandwich from a platter in the dining room, poured cold beer into a thin old pewter mug, and went up the stairs to her bedroom trying not to look as if she were running away from anything or anybody.

From behind Sophie's half-closed door, the eternal communion with the telephone. ''. . . Yes, love, soon, soon . . .'' and a soft gust of warmth, passion, passed across the landing. Who? Who was Sophie's soon, soon love? Something about the voice, the spilled-out emotion, gave her a sense of great loneliness, coldness. Not wanting to hear any more, or to be heard hearing, she closed her own door soundlessly.

No, not running away; just a quiet interlude, a catching of the breath, in which perhaps to read a chapter or so of Trollope's *Barchester Towers*. And come back to her center, from wherever the various portions had been blown and scattered.

There were too many people outside to use the lawn and the garden as a retreat. She was weary of acknowledging sympathies, listening to recollections, and seeing the unspoken fascinated questions in the eyes: he must have left an awful lot of money?—how will it be divided up?—does it just go to his brothers and sister, or—?

The moors as a place to disappear for a time had lost their appeal. Since . . . this *morning?* Yes, this morning.

And the normal-abnormal lunchtime sounds in the house itself . . .

Water running in the kitchen, the reassuring peaceful clatter of silver spoons and forks and knives as they were replaced in slotted drawers.

Marcia, to Leo: "You should have some hot soup, you look positively green, Leo, I wonder about your liver. . . ."

Pitch, the black cat, jumping up on the dining room table and Sophie saying, before she ran up the stairs, "He'll be curlin' up on the caviar sandwiches next, down! you Stygian beast."

Everybody by now seemed to be taking Phip, lying under his light-trembled windows, deep in his flowers, for granted.

Except for the occasional black windy moment when you let reality lay its hands on you, mortality—

Fingers would pause midway in the act of lighting a cigarette. A sentence, started enthusiastically, would falter and stop and then with an effort of will be picked up.

And the eyes sought petals, light, faces, living faces, and the ears tuned themselves to voices, laughter, hungrily recording even the clock's ticking and the scuttering sound of the wind in the aspens. *I'm alive.*

Trying to concentrate on her book, Kate fought the lost, bereft feeling.

Well, she was bereft. From the early Anglo-Saxon, if she remembered correctly, deprived, dispossessed, made destitute. An overstatement, but—

"You're a warm woman, Kate. You'd make a nice wife. . . ." The last things he had ever said to her.

There was a quick crisp knock on her door. She opened it to Jack.

"May I come in for a moment? I know you're tired of everybody, I can't say I blame you, go back and sit down, what are you reading?"

With the liveliest curiosity, he picked up the little dark blue Oxford University Press edition of Trollope. "I haven't read this for ten years." A flash of merriment on his face. "The Bishop. And Mrs. Proudie. And la Signora Madeline Vesey Neroni, and Bertie Stanhope saying he'd been a Jew once. Mr. Slope adding an *e* to his name for the sake of euphony. . . ."

Amazing to feel so close to someone, so charmingly at home, over a thumbed cherished book.

A nice safe subject in this odd moment of being alone in a houseful of people; books. "Neither have I, for years, I mean," Kate said, "so I thought the time was ripe again." She went back to her lavender and white flowered chair by the window.

He more than filled the little slant-eaved room. It crackled with him. He came over and half leaned, half sat on the high broad window sill.

She followed his invading eyes, his gaze moving, pausing, here and there, in her private place. Her robe, dark sapphire silk, hanging rakishly and shapelessly by one shoulder seam from the hook inside the bedroom door. Slippers beside the bed, embroidered silk ones sent by Livia from Hong Kong, one right side up and one upside down.

The bed, broad, headboard and footboard of highly polished brass, old sumptuous random patchwork quilt of silks and satins and taffetas, like a toss of jewels; but primly and crisply made up now, the sleeper with her long loose abandonment of hair up and combed and armed for the day.

A few wild asters she had picked, yesterday afternoon, ashy lavender, in a crystal tumbler beside the bed, together with a spray of tiny starry white daisies that had instantly perished when the hand had snapped their stem.

A little powder spilled on the dressing table. A bottle she hadn't properly closed, faintly letting its scent of tuberoses escape. A necklace she had decided against, last night, emerald-green glass beads, slung over the handle of the closet door.

This exploration took him perhaps half an absorbed second.

He turned his head to her.

"Am I cast into outer darkness, then, Kate?"

She felt as if she were too close to an open fire and wanted to move away, and kept herself very still, hands folded loosely in her lap.

Surely his face was four or five feet away and not as close as it seemed? The big raking Converse nose, the intent eyes that seemed to pour a bath of blue light over her, the flicker of muscles in the strong smooth throat as he said—

What had he said?

"Outer darkness? What does that mean?"

He reached down and very lightly disengaged one of her hands from the other and stroked the back of it gently with his thumb. She listened to two voices, one his touch, the other saying, with just the faintest suggestion of laughter behind it, "Look, Kate. After you finish your day's work in New York, I don't imagine you take up den mothering for the Murray Hill troop of the Girl Scouts. Or enter baking contests, or get in a good stint at your embroidery hoop. And I'm sure you don't think that when I'm sprung I devote my spare time to studying the Russian language—although I'm working at it a bit—or improving my backstroke at the Y."

Yes, much too close to the fire, she could feel the heat of it coloring her face.

"You're very articulate so far, will you finish what it is you're trying to tell me?"

"Your, Sophie's words, Latin lover da Gama—sorry, di Castro—burns up the Bell System, and I still regard you with the greatest friendship and esteem. But Eugenia comes around these premises and spills endearments in public, and you snap your shade down in my face."

After a moment, she said, "You do paint a ghastly picture of me. I hadn't realized. I thought we were sort of Hansel and Gretel keeping each other warm. Thank you for putting things so objectively in focus." Resisting a desire to snatch, she removed her hand from his.

As though she hadn't spoken, he said, "But for the moment, stay with me, will you? I need you and I think you need me right now. We can sort the four of us out later. If you insist. If you think it will even be necessary. You probably know things I don't know, about what's happening here, around us, you're the only one I can talk to without getting some kind of evasion or raised fist or biblical insult. Either it's all a bad dream, or, as Sophie would say, a crock of the well-known article—or afterthoughts, guilt—*or* someone here has managed two sudden deaths, or at least one, in one short week."

The strange, the impossible words hung on the still air. He waited almost anxiously for dismissing laughter, or a mocking incredulous repetition of the words. She was silent, not looking at him, thick lashes doing their basic work of screening.

"When I say it out loud, it sounds just as mad to me as it does to you. And if it did happen, it's probably going to be buried for good and all tomorrow, in nomine Patris, et Filii, et Spiritus Sancti. Oh, and in Spiggott's grave, or crematory, too. But this house isn't a good place any more, or a safe place to go away by yourself in, or keep your secrets in."

Kate listened and at the same time made a large and successful effort within herself. Leave the litter of emotion, not entirely comprehended. Come back to life and death and now.

"Then you're going to pass, too?"

"I'm not a crusading saint," he said almost angrily, getting up and striding the room. "What the hell can I do in any case?" He seemed to be talking more to himself than to her. "I'm Judas, I'm the asp in their bosom, I'm just up here covering a story—five minutes ago Garrett said to me, 'You'd destroy Phip too? A lewd old man fumbling with the fastenings of his housekeeper's corsets?' "

His skin was a curious deep red. Rage, distress, frustration, or all of them?

"And what was your answer to that?" Kate said steadily.

"I said I saw nothing wrong with love, affection, any time, any age, there's not enough of it to go round as it is. He takes a somewhat one-sided view, naturally. I have his script written for him, roughly as follows. He probably has his letter of resignation ready, you can't fire me, I quit. One of our great-aunts left him a house in Dublin, on Stephen's Green, he can live comfortably there on Phip. Handsome rogues go over well in more civilized countries than this. . . . But where were we? Yes, I pass. I think.''

He came over and picked her up out of her chair. There was in him an immense need she could feel pouring at her. He kissed her with an astonished passion that just stopped short of hurting, his body greeting, explicit, against hers.

He said into her hair, ''You make a delightful Gretel, Kate.''

The door opened, casually and without haste. Eugenia stood watching them.

Arms, warmth, dropped away from Kate.

''I'm so sorry,'' Eugenia said. ''I heard your voice and came up to say I must run—mustn't intrude further.''

She did Kate, head to foot, in one glance.

''How sweet, family affection, a disappearing commodity.''

Kate had never imagined him at a loss, as he was now. From his distance of about eight inches from her, she felt his unhappiness, and his difficulty in producing polite words for the three of them to hear.

''Nice of you to stop by, Eugenia.''

Leave them alone; let them repair themselves in decent privacy.

She made an abrupt move toward the door and he caught her wrist in a powerful tightening hand.

''It started out by being intended to be nice,'' Eugenia said. There was a sound to her voice of a flag snapping in the wind. ''But one way or another, it may have been profitable too.''

A meeting of two pairs of blue eyes, a swift turn releasing a gust of Je Reviens, and over her shoulder as she started down the stairway, ''To hell with the Marquis of Queensberry rules from here on in.''

TWENTY

"I think," Kate said carefully, "we'd better go downstairs."

"I think you're right. One way or another this room seems to be seething with sex." He had recovered himself; he looked thoughtful, his mind obviously on Eugenia. "You never did get at your *Barchester Towers.* . . ."

"Telephone for you, Kate," Timothy called from the lower hall.

"Give him my regards," Jack said, on his way to the door, "or better still tell him your line is busy." He felt something in the air behind him; tingling, winy. Joyousness?

A voice with the soft broad *a* of the Cape said, "This is Mabel Breen, you don't know me, I'm Stella Grahn's sister, I think it would be to our mutual advantage if you could come to my house, right now, and if you know what's good for you and your family don't tell anyone about it."

It sounded rehearsed, spilled uncertainly out; the effect was of an aggressive kind of timidity.

"But what—?"

"I can't talk. Stell says the house is full of phones. One eleven Kimball Street in P-town. I'll be expecting you."

Looking back, she wondered at her readiness to accept the invitation, or demand. But it had occurred to her that it might be something about Sophie, and her presence in North Truro last Sunday. Or about matters far worse, told to her in detail by her sister.

There was the outside chance that Mabel Breen wanted to be of help; or just eager to move onto the stage, into the drama.

Concerning her own selection, she thought she might reasonably be taken as the least formidable of the Converse females.

From Phip's office, Leo's groan: "My God, a whole salmon from Canada, for him, and a wheel of Wisconsin cheddar, I forgot his birthday is next week—and will you kindly help yourself to *The Times* of London and the *Manchester Guardian* and—"

Kate put her head in at the door. "May I borrow your car, Jack? An errand in Provincetown."

He was thankfully clutching an armful of newspapers. "Yes, of course, here—" He handed her his ignition key and gave her an X-ray gaze; she was unaware of her own rosiness and shimmer.

Mabel Breen's house was a brown bungalow, with interior darkness guaranteed not only by the building style but by screened porches and muffling cedars. It looked safe, drab, and depressingly ordinary. And, a sunny day, people coming and going on Kimball Street, a tricycle parked merrily on the cement front walk. Nothing to be frightened of, surely.

Action was a sort of tonic in any case. She hadn't realized the density of the air in Phip's house, the watching of words, the unsettling glances, eyes flicking away when you met them, except for those blue, owning ones; a choking unformulated kind of suspicion . . . who, which one, why, impossible—

Healthy to get away from Jack, too. And assess what it was, pressing your nose against Cartier's window, seeing some splendid fiery glow, thinking in a moment of abandonment, fantasy, If it's all that marvelous it must be for me.

On the lawn, "For Christ's sake, Eugenia—" The voice not, entirely, husbandly; but she read into the tone bed and lazy breakfasts and shared showers.

You make a delightful Gretel, Kate.

Mabel Breen, answering her knock, looked like someone in an old late night movie. Her hair was teased and sprayed into an unlikely feathery ball, pink-blond, dark at the roots, probably colored at home. She wore a heavily dragoned black kimono and gold mules. Her face was long, thin, sallow, and disappointed.

"Come in," she said. "Just to your right there." She sounded as she had over the telephone, timid but a little threatening.

Her front room looked like the waiting room of an unsuccessful dentist, matched pieces of maple veneer, cretonne cushions tied on, a highly varnished coffee table holding mathematically arranged magazines, a tired dark green broadloom rug, a crowd of little pots of philodendron and cactus on the window sills. It was very dark.

Look invulnerable. Look in command of yourself and whatever situation this was going to be. Kate sat down in one of the cretonne-cushioned chairs. She lit a cigarette with a leisurely flick of her lighter. "Well, Mrs. Breen, what is it, I have a number of things to see to before I drive back."

Mabel Breen sat down on the edge of the maple love seat facing her. She gazed not at but past her visitor's eyes, which was unnerving. To a cactus in a miniature whale-shaped pot she said, "When it first happened Stell was beside herself. She called me from his house at some ungodly hour, she was crying so hard she couldn't hardly talk. After a while she got herself together. And that was the end of her telling me things, her own sister. I doubt she even remembers what she said, that night, hysterical, she was—"

Kate felt frozen in position, unable even to flick the very long ash from her cigarette into a tray that said "Souvenir of Provincetown" and had a badly painted Pilgrim Monument on it.

Of course, she should have known.

Had there been some idea at the back of her head, Kate conquers all? Everything's all right, I've seen the sister and it's after all nothing, relax, everybody.

But if she had refused to come, something even more unpleasant than this long, long silence while she hunted for safe words might conceivably have happened.

What would crisp executive Kate do? She opened her handbag and took out a little red leather address book and removed the tiny silver pencil from its spine. "If you don't mind talking slowly . . . I want to get this down. Yes . . . mmmm . . . let's see, 'I doubt she even remembers what she—' "

In a sudden frightening move, Mabel Breen leaned across and snatched the address book from her hand. "Don't you dare write nothing down."

So much for executive Kate.

"I thought it would be a favor to you, letting you know that someone else knows, even though Stell might have forgotten."

Knows what? Impossible to ask and let the words shape themselves into some enormous, unhandleable statement.

Oh hell, Kate thought wearily. "Knows what, Mrs. Breen?"

The mouth pursed itself. "I'm not prepared to say until you tell me you're going to co-operate. On behalf of the *Converses*." Something about the way she spoke the family name told a great deal. Jealousy of her sister's job, the moneyed world she moved in, the daily life set about with luxuries, unlimited miles away from this dismal parlor.

How much was she going to ask for? Twenty-five thousand, one hundred thousand?

"Do give me back my address book," she said, reaching out her hand, calm over an inner trembling.

Whatever she said next would probably be the fatally wrong thing; she had no experience of criminal doings.

"Perhaps we'd better go directly from here to the police station, if you think you have any information of vital importance about my uncle's death."

"No! Not the police, Stell would kill me"—fear in the sour dark eyes. It was clear which of the sisters dominated.

Mabel Breen's own hands were trembling. "Here's your book back. She has—or make it *had*—everything. You ought to see the bedroom she slept in. Oh, of course, you're there, in that house— And going on and on about the things she cooked, the wines she'd pour into her pots, and the house in New York, two maids at her beck and call, and a chauffeur, and he sent her for a week to Bermuda last May when she'd had a virus. . . ."

"Yes," Kate prompted gently, into the silence.

"He's left her an annuity, twenty-five hundred dollars a year for the rest of her life. And," almost as an afterthought, "he was going to marry her." She hugged herself into her kimono, bent over. "Mr. Breen, my husband that is, left me last year, I suppose you all know about that, she's gotten in the way of thinking *she's* one of the family."

A remark that fell sadly on the air; as though any of them gave a damn about Mrs. Grahn's sister's husband.

"Yes, marry her, and then she'd really have the chauffeur and the maids and the two houses. And he was a nice man, young for his age."

Push away the panic. Have another cigarette. She had given up smoking a month ago.

"As I said, Mrs. Breen, if you'll change we'd better go to the police." She felt safer, this time, with her threat.

". . . but you can't tell me, with all that money, they'd miss it—"

"Miss what?"

"I think it's called Haverford. She showed it to me. She said, We eat off it just as if it was everyday. And he has three other sets just for this house *here*. The Haverford has rosebuds on it, and a gold edge, real gold, Stell says. It's a service for eight. There's a platter that goes along with it too, and a gravy boat. They'll be breaking up that place anyway, relatives grabbing this and that, so I thought . . ."

She was breathless, as though the effort of making her demand clear was almost too much for her.

Kate listened to the sound of the clock on the mantelpiece, shaped like a ship's wheel, and watched reflected light glide across the ceiling as a small girl, outside the window, collected her tricycle from the front walk.

Blackmail turning out to be a service of Haviland china.

Refuse? Blackmailers, traditionally, kept it up after you gave in the first time, relentlessly continuing their hold on you. Today the Haviland, tomorrow the world. Jack darling, practical tough Jack, what would you do?

In defiance of all the rules of a game she didn't know, and relying on her own understanding of this possibly dangerous but somehow pathetic woman, she said, "There are more things in that house than we know what to do with, and we're all up to here in china."

She scribbled, in her little book: "Received from Katherine Converse, one set of Haviland china as a present from Mr. P. A. Converse's estate, as Mrs. B. told Mr. C. she particularly admired this set."

"Sign this, please."

"I don't want to sign anything—"

"Just," Kate said patiently, "so the rest of the family knows whom it's to go to and it's not carted off to New York by accident."

Her argument would not have convinced her, but it seemed to sound plausible to Mabel Breen. She wrote her name in slow Palmer Method, added the date, and said uncertainly, "Will you have a cup of coffee? Or tea?"

"No, thanks, I must be off. Have you a car or shall I see that it's delivered to you?"

"Oh, delivered, please—" She shivered, either in nervous reaction, or in fear. "I wouldn't want to go anywhere near that house."

Something about her voice made Kate add a mental codicil to her bill of lading. "You see, Sergeant, I thought this woman might spread a lot of horrible cooked-up gossip and it seemed the least I could do for my uncle. He never cared about *things* anyway, he just sort of accumulated them. . . ."

As she drove away she realized that she hadn't discovered at all what Mrs. Mabel Breen knew, beyond the fact of the impending marriage. Which could be true, or just her sister's boasting.

Congratulations, Kate, a resonant and sardonic voice said in her ear. Only two or three, or four or five stones left unturned. You're wasted in advertising, you ought to work for the FBI.

Well, he didn't have to know about it, it was strictly between her and Mrs. Breen.

In the MG, Tike said through her teeth to Robbin Roy, "That sneaky bitch was in there almost half an hour. And just blind luck that I spotted his Ford in front."

"Maybe they're old friends, sweetie."

"I don't see how they could be, *I* never laid eyes on Grahn's sister, I only knew the house because once when her car was out of gas Uncle Phip made me drive her there to play pinochle. Between her and Jack, they're going to, like, louse us all up for good. Keep your fingers crossed until 10 A.M. tomorrow, once he's buried he's buried."

TWENTY-ONE

"Your turn on the blower, Vin," Sophie said. "I'd hate for you to feel left out of things."

Vin put down his gin on the rocks and walked with a deliberate betraying care to the telephone. He said very little. He listened for a while, color surging up under his immaculate red-and-white-striped collar, the knuckles of his hand prominent, holding the receiver.

He seemed gradually to sag, to fold into himself in a way that reminded Kate of Mabel Breen hugging deep into her kimono, saying her husband had left her, she supposed they all knew about it.

Glenna said in a voice a little above a whisper, "Oh God, I can't—"

"For better or for worse, last I heard," Sophie said. "In sickness and in health, and also in the event of a mate's bein' screwed blind." She, too, watched Vin. He had hung up and stood motionless, his head bent.

She went over to him and put a hand on his shoulder. There was a single great convulsive heave, a gout of tears on a face you wanted to look in decency away from, and then he stood up straight and quietly and formally dried his eyes and his cheeks with his handkerchief.

As though he were a tape recorder playing back, he recited to the room in his deep, rich voice, "Afternoon, Vin, Toby Towers here. I've been reading in the newspapers about your

good fortune—in addition to your great personal grief and loss,
I mean—and I hope it won't be out of the way for me to offer
congratulations. It must be nice to have money but I mean
money in the family. This seems as good a time as any to say
we're buttoning down the budget, business conditions . . .
well, you know, you're an old stager, teach your grandfather
to suck dollar bills. . . . In any case, the board decided this
morning the time is ripe for your separation from the company,
bad thing to lose a man of your long experience but I suppose
you're able now to think of being a, what do they call it,
gentleman of leisure—''

And patiently clarifying matters, he said, "Fired." And
looked at the still, pink face of his uncle ten feet away and
said tightly, jocularly, "Move over, Phip."

"Let's," Sophie said, "go in a body—oh, sorry—and get
coffee and I don't know anythin' nicer than a sediment of
brandy in the bottom of it, Vin darlin'—"

Glenna had moved to his side. "I'll take care of my husband."

"I'd been sort of hopin' you would arise to that challenge.
Kitchen, y'all."

Mrs. Grahn was at the rear of the pantry, pouring hot paraffin
on top of her glasses of beach plum jelly, a dark silhouette
against the screen. Her usual immense pot of fresh coffee puffed
steam, on the black iron stove.

As they converged on the ordinariness, the cheer of the
kitchen, it seemed surprising to nobody but Kate that an arm
went around her waist, casually, electrically.

Then the arm tightened in an absent-minded way until she
felt she could scarcely breathe. She followed his bolted gaze
to the slate that hung by the door leading to the back. It was
used by Mrs. Grahn to note down groceries and commodities
freshly run out of, so that she could remember to order them.

On it was written in white chalk, "scouring powder, bleach."
And underneath that, in what looked to be another and possibly
a disguised left-handed sort of printing, "Vin did it," each of
the three words crudely underlined three times.

Jack said nothing, but a feelable recoil, or shock, emanated
from him and suddenly they were all looking at the slate.

Pitch meowed at the door to be let in.

Glenna backed slowly to the sink, seized a sponge, walked toward the door, and with a lightning swipe erased the slate.

Vin started to laugh, a sound in his nose without any kind of merriment. There were other voices, other noises, an inarticulate growl from Leo, a sibilant "Jesus Christ" from Sophie.

"Mrs. Grahn," Jack said, "this slate — would you mind — did you see anything added to your scouring powder and bleach, or did you make another note for yourself?"

She came slowly out of the pantry. "No, and I don't thank whoever wiped off that slate, with all the things I've got on my mind, big and little. . . . I've been busy with my jelly in there the better part of an hour, what did they put, what did they write, on my slate?"

"It said, 'Vin did it.' " Tike's voice clear and high from her lounging pose in the living room door frame. "Mr. Vincent Converse, that is."

Jack was alarmed at Vin's face. He went to him and took his arm.

"You want air—"

He flung the back door open and Vin followed him out into the sharply cooling, darkening afternoon.

In a sleepwalking way, Vin said, "Of course. I'm a natural, if it's a killer that's got to be offered up here in this house, some kind of sacrifice to appease something or other."

Both hands were deep in his pockets, Jack thought probably to hide their trembling. "Poor lost Vin. Fucking old flop, more accurately put. Pin the tail on the donkey and get on with it."

"Look, Vin, it's not that easy to nail the donkey. If it's not just a piece of idle malice, all you have to do is place yourself elsewhere. Physically. On Tuesday, I mean. God knows whose name will show up next, after you've removed yourself from the list."

"I had one of those countless Arabian nights of the advertising man," Vin said. There was pain in his voice, and something that sounded like fear. "Clients, drinks, girls here and there, more drinks, a part of town I usually avoid but they wanted to have a nice pigging time of it. . . . As usual, after a certain amount of liquor, the remainder of the night was a blank, which up till now I found myself grateful for.''

"Well, still easy. Your credit card—''

"My wallet was neatly removed, in the elevator at Jesup on Monday. I keep a hunk of cash for emergencies in a safe in my office.''

"But Glenna—?''

"We had a fight. She went off to her mother's and came home to find me gracefully prone on the living room sofa, sometime after nine, a new cigarette burn on the rug— Do you happen to have a pair of handcuffs on you, friend?''

The shock, the pain, were getting a brave coating of Vin's fabled jauntiness. It crossed Jack's mind that a possible line of defense, a script for Vin's Tuesday night, might be being tried out on him, to see how it went down.

"Don't be a damned fool, we're all in this together,'' he said harshly, taken aback by his own fleeting thought and deeply concerned for Vin.

Vin, moving or being pushed to some kind of dangerous desperate edge; and in an indefinable way, big as he was, and still able to summon resources of strength as he was now doing, destroyed.

"I think it's more than time for me to reunite myself with my glass,'' Vin said. "If you'll excuse me. And not through that kitchen, with that woman in it. And that slate. I suppose the police have a way of recovering chalk erasures, don't you?''

He walked, very erect and very alone, around the corner of the house.

Jack, needing Kate, went back into the kitchen. The tableau of his relatives remained in position, except that Sophie in graceful motion was handing cups of coffee around.

"Well, did he, Jack?'' Tike asked brightly, tongue flicking her mouth corner, eager.

"Did he what? Need some air? Yes.'' And something about her hungrily expectant face prompting him, "Did you write that, on the slate? It seems a Tike thing to do. Although I don't know why I know. I never knew you well enough before to dislike you.''

Unused to open male rejection, Tike said spitefully, "Maybe

Kate can, like, clear things up. She paid a long visit to Mrs. Grahn's sister today. They may have been just discussing the weather or something all that time, but it seems queer, doesn't it?''

Kate felt the impact of eyes.

"Not the weather," she said calmly. "We were discussing china. Mrs. Grahn's sister is very interested in china, particularly Haviland."

There was a polite knock at the back door. It opened and a delivery boy came in, jeans, nylon jacket, staring brown eyes, pink acned skin, and immense cardboard box. He thumped it down on the oak table, looked around shyly but with an avid curiosity, and lighting on a safe familiar face, said, "Afternoon, Mrs. Grahn. Too bad about Mr. Spiggott, isn't it? Nice fella. . . ."

"Too bad *what* about Mr. Spiggott?" Mrs. Grahn asked slowly.

"Well, I thought you'd heard, I just heard on the way out of the store—he's dead, and not far from here, they say, round about Highland Light, but down on the beach, fell over the edge, they say—"

In a convulsive physical reaction, Mrs. Grahn's arm shot out as if grasping for some support. Her hand hit a huge blue pot on the back burner and it flew into the air. A chicken stew in wine erupted and, splashing on the floor, found one of Garrett's English-wooleened ankles. He cried out with pain, but the sound was all but drowned by Mrs. Grahn's rising scream.

"Dead? Fell? When? Right after he came here, to this house? Wanting a private talk with that man there?" She pointed a trembling finger at Leo.

The delivery boy, eyes even wider, fascinated, muttered, "Sometime in the night, they say. Accident, they say."

"Murderers!" screamed Mrs. Grahn from the bottom of her diaphragm, the voice seeming to make the kitchen walls shake. "One of you, all of you, *murderers—*"

She looked for a moment as if she was going to faint and then, "Don't you move, you, Jonathan Spiller, you wait for me, I'm getting out of this house, not another bed made, not another dish cooked, I'll be the next one, him in there between his candles and now poor Tom Spiggott, you can take me to the police, I don't dare to drive my own car because for all I know they've put a bomb in the engine to blow me up, God help anyone who gets in their way—''

As if beginning to catch the heady disease of hysteria, Glenna got up from the rocker she had collapsed into after washing the slate clean.

Her voice started out hard and crisp but much too fast.

''Just wait a minute, Mrs. Grahn, just you wait a minute.''

She looked deliberately about the room, mouth in bitter lines. ''You're all so bright, you're all so smart, senators and lawyers and reporters and models and advertising executives— Yes, Vin's down, give him a kick while it's handy, say if anyone did it he did it—''

''Thanks for skippin' the haute couture,'' Sophie murmured almost inaudibly, looking very pale, and putting down her coffee cup and saucer on the table to get rid of the tiny clattering hand-shaking noise.

''—But has it occurred to any of you that this good house-keeping soul might have done it?'' Voice high, shrill, edged with tears; but collected indictments. ''Maybe this whole story of hers, Phip, murder, is because she killed him and thought someone else might find out and she wanted to be in the clear. Maybe he was going to fire her and change his will the *other* way around—you told me, didn't you, Leo, that she gets a nice little annuity? Maybe she gave him the wrong medicine, or didn't give him the right medicine, who's to say, who'd know, and maybe Spiggott knew she wasn't playing cards with her sister at all and came around here and—''

''This minute,'' Mrs. Grahn said. ''Out of this house this minute, Jonathan Spiller.''

Under the echoes of Glenna's cry, and into the appalled silence, she said, ''I can't think where my pocketbook is—oh yes, in the pantry—this *minute*.''

No one, except Mrs. Grahn and the Spiller boy, seemed capable of movement. The two left by the back door, so well hinged and oiled that it refused to slam. There was the sound of the delivery truck starting up.

Leo said ferociously, ''Congratulations on sending that

woman, finally, into action, Glenna.''

Glenna burst into tears, as alone against her wall as Vin had been, Jack thought, going around the corner of the house, back to his drink.

Where was Vin? Hadn't he heard his wife's tormented counterattack?

He appeared beyond Tike, in the doorway, voice thick and soft.

"Yes," he said to Jack, family esp, "I heard it. Thanks, Glenna, for trying to find someone else. I was just in there, sitting with Phip, you know, wondering what it's, what anything's, all about, and thinking that perhaps, seeing this is the way you end up, it doesn't matter, actually. The captains and the kings depart—who said that, I forget. Anyway, darling, I think it's time I took you across the street.''

Glenna, looking exhausted, looking older, in spite of her tennis and all those lengths in the pool, said, "Yes, Vin. Yes, please.''

TWENTY-TWO

Most of the people who wished to pay their respects to Phip had come and gone.

The flowers had been halved by Marcia before her afternoon nap and driven by Timothy to the hospital in Hyannis. Tike saw him just before he left, in Vin's Cadillac, coppery dark face and neck among shafts of gladioli, explosions of roses and carnations, chrysanthemums and more roses, on front and back seats and floor.

"You look like the living dead, driving yourself to your own funeral," she gasped, clutching her ribs with laughter.

While in Hyannis, Timothy mailed a large flat package to himself in New York, parcel post.

As the afternoon darkened, there was a not very subtle change in the aggregate character of the mourners. Nobody could say for sure whether or not they were acquaintances of Phip's, nodding friends, people he did business with or to whom he had been kind; but there was an air of driving curiosity about them, and a feeling that some spectacle was to be seen before it was too late.

Marcia, for a while, politely coped, listened to the "Sorry for your trouble," which is an automatic way to announce your connection with the deceased, your right to be there; no identification needed.

Kate and Sophie helped. There was something alarming about the greedy eyes, the silence except in far corners where people muttered to each other.

Five boys who Kate thought would be described on paper

as youths came in together, leaving their high hard laughter just outside the front door. Jeaned and booted, leather-jacketed, creaking, and smelling of motorcycle oil. A little whirl of violence on the air entered with them. They gave her a casually insulting comprehensive look, as if she were a piece of merchandise on display for their approval; and went and stood by the coffin and gazed down at Phip, making a great show of blessing themselves.

"*Looks* all right, don't he?" one boy said. Kate went into the kitchen and summoned Jack away from his peaceful rocker and his *Times* of London.

The boys had invaded the dining room and were pouring immense scotches into Waterford crystal. Jack stood for a second or two watching them, formidable, unsmiling.

"Down the hatch," he said. "Although you look to be under age. Very kind of you to come around. A bit late, however, special family services are about to begin, if you don't mind."

There was a hesitation, a tinkering with the idea of some game to be played.

One boy giggled. "They say he got it, like." He took a large swallow of J and B and choked on it. "Here's to crime, like they say."

Jack took away his glass and, propelling him by the shoulders, ejected him through the open front door. Turning, he said to the other four, "Out."

Another menacing hesitation, until Leo loomed in the living room doorway. Then defiantly, shooting their drinks down their throats, they exchanged hard stares with both Converses and left abruptly.

"Good party the fella throws," one boy tossed back. "Too bad he's not alive to join the fun. We weren't going to stay anyway, we heard this place isn't, like, healthy, or anywhere around here, Highland Light, like. . . ."

"I think"—Leo glanced at his watch—"we may allow ourselves a drink. And then I'll put a rude sign on the front door. Private, family only, something like that. I suppose you know we've been getting what are known as thrill-seekers?"

"Sorry, I'm ashamed to say I've been hiding. Yes, another ounce, Leo, while you're at it. And pour one for Kate and one for Sophie."

He looked carefully at Kate, as if checking to see that brows and lashes, eyes and mouth, were all correct. Her face was drawn and shadowed.

"I suppose Vin's resting?" Her eyes went to Sophie in a way he didn't understand: worried, angry.

"I suppose so, or holding Glenna's hand or feeding her tranquilizers."

"Do you think there could be anything in what she said?"

"I don't know, and from here I'm not sure anyone will ever know," Jack said in a voice that was tired and uncertain, out of character. "About any of it, that is."

"You don't suppose those boys will come back and give this wake a colorful conclusion? Ropes and knives, rape and robbery, the works?"

"No. And you're not entirely alone, you know." He sensed the tremble of genuine fear of something, under the light question, and regretted various pairs of eyes on them. "Leo's going to lock up in a few minutes in any case."

His gaze lit on what was to be the last of the mourners admitted to the house: a stocky man in his thirties, red hair, freckles, expensive suit in Stewart plaid, which when he rose from the kneeler showed itself to be vested in white linen.

He went over to him and said, "Jenkins, isn't it? We met years ago."

"Yes, Peter Jenkins." They shook hands without enthusiasm on either side. "Sad thing."

"Let's see, you're with the Boston affiliate of the network, now, I forget your call letters at the moment. . . ."

"Well, that's it." Jenkins grinned happily. "We once did a television interview with him on his Hearth Homes, right here in this room, he was sitting over there by the fireplace, quite a big man in these parts, you know. I took a fancy to him, he gave the whole crew drinks and dinner and we had a hell of a good time."

"Nice of you to come all this way. Have you by any chance seen Eugenia?"

Jenkins looked past him. "Not yet, I might buzz her later, in Provincetown."

"Where, in Provincetown?"

"At the Inn, if I recall rightly."

"She didn't suggest that you come out here?"

Jenkins was a cameraman for the Boston station as well as being an old friend of Eugenia's; and, Jack thought, had probably been a lover for what Eugenia airily called a short spin.

"Good Lord, man, do you have to have a written invitation to say an Our Father and a Hail Mary? I'll have a quick drink if I may and then remove the body. Oh—excuse me. And as for coming all this way, I can't take credit for that, I often weekend in P-town when the striped bass are running."

This is not after all, Kate finally told herself, recollecting Jack's half-teasing voice in her bedroom, the Murray Hill troop of the Girl Scouts.

When Sophie left the room, she followed her up the stairs and went in and sat down on Mrs. Grahn's favorite chair, by the window, down-cushioned apple-green silk. Sophie sat down at the little enameled dressing table and got to work in a leisurely manner on her face.

"First," she said in a department store demonstrating manner, "we remove the stains and strains of the day, thus." A cream that smelled of limes, cleansing tissues gently employed. "Now we neutralize, dear," shaking a thin clear liquid onto cotton pads and patting them lightly over her skin.

"Sophie . . ."

"What's on your mind? Besides death and transfiguration, and possibly side trips down shady lanes in green and pleasant woods, with the First Prize?"

The eyes in the mirror chose not to meet hers. With delicately flying fingertips, Sophie spread a sheer fine bloom of no color at all.

She was feathering it onto her chin and throat when Kate said, "I'm sorry, Sophie, but it's not fair. To see Vin whipped and wounded . . . and alone . . ."

"Mercy, how dramatic. And not alone, he has a spouse of sorts. No, that's not kind, but she certainly took her time to rally round the flag."

Kate went on stubbornly, "I seem to get the feeling that everybody thinks if it has to be someone it might as well be Vin, he's well cast for the script— I heard Jule, Sophie. I heard her say you were up here last Sunday. You've never said a word about it.''

"Meanin' you're now castin' me for a part?''

There was a little stinging silence in the room.

"Put the window down, if you will,'' Sophie said. "Weather's changin', it's chilly.''

"No, I didn't mean that at all. But why should you hug that to yourself when it looks as if he's the only one who might land in trouble?''

"Okay,'' Sophie said. "I like you and I trust you, and this is for your shell-like ears alone. I needed money, lots of green foldin' money, things at Sophie Converse, Inc., took a colossal turn for the worse, business bein' what it is. I didn't want to go to the banks and they might not have been all that happy at coughin' up. And the minute word gets out—to borrow a cliché of our leaders in Washington, the domino theory, mine would begin topplin' at a telescoped rate. Gossip, dirty talk, is it true what they say about Dixie? The buzzards gather and swoop. And before you know it, everythin' I've done with my life is over and out. Sunk without a trace.''

Now she did, anxiously, arrange a meeting of eyes in the mirror, studying Kate's.

"It would have come to me anyway in the natural course of events. God-blessed Phip said, Sure, Sophie—''

"And he gave it to you?''

"He was to mail me a check this week, even Croesuses don't keep vast sums lyin' idle to write the occasional check on. And in addition to my dominoes, word gettin' out, I have an uncomfortable helpin' of southern pride with this particular family, name of Converse.''

Of course. Her father. She sounded for a moment like a cold and angry stranger.

It was a perfectly rational explanation. But Kate felt without knowing why that Sophie was holding something back. Or twisting something around.

"Your face will get you in trouble some day,'' Sophie said very softly. "It reads, easily. You're sayin', But she just gave herself one hell of a motive for murder if *he* said, Sorry, Sophie, my girl friend's in the picture now and I'm in the process of readjustin' my estate.'' A wave of color came up under her translucent skin. ''Well, Kate, there's nothin' more I can add, except maybe you'd be wise to get out of here, lightnin' can strike twice in the same place, can't it, and come to think of it I'm bigger than you are—''

Kate got up and went over to her and bent down and kissed the hot cheek. She couldn't speak but she hoped Sophie got her message. Yes, something's wrong, something's left out, Sophie, but I can't believe it, I don't believe it . . . at all . . . not you, Sophie. Not you, disposing of Phip.

As she turned to leave the room Sophie put her head into her hands and began weeping into her beautiful fresh makeup. Tension under control too long? Grief accumulated, finally pouring out? Champagne?

She hesitated in the doorway, but Sophie's shoulders and back said, Leave me alone.

TWENTY-THREE

Thinking about a possibly hot exchange over the telephone, Jack went across the street to call Eugenia. As he passed the stair well on the way out of the house, he stopped for a moment and listened to the muted, closed-door weeping above. Somebody trying to finish up with it—gasping, a cough—Sophie.

Well, people did weep, in the presence of death. The memory of the sound followed him into his room. Before hearing about Mr. Spiggott, before her flight, Mrs. Grahn had gone through it like a clean wind; it was ordered and immaculate, bed taut, clothes hung up, ashtray glistening.

He wondered, not for the first time, if the efficient fingers explored pockets and dresser drawers.

Jenkins had been right. She was at the Provincetown Inn.

"Eugenia? I thought you were tethered in Hyannisport."

"Well, I will be tomorrow, but it seemed not . . . thoughtful when your uncle's to be buried in the morning, to be this close and . . . Naturally, I'll just slip into the church for the service and out, I won't go on to the cemetery."

"Has Peter Jenkins looked you up yet?"

Smooth; prepared, he thought. "Who? Oh, Peter. If he wants me to surf-cast he's got the wrong girl."

"I think I'd better talk to you. In person."

"How lovely, in person."

"About the Marquis of Queensberry rules, that is."

"Oh, has that been bothering you? What I meant was that

you're not only fetching and talented *but* will be rich and I'm
not about to abandon you to that cousin . . . very attractive-
looking creature, but all the wrong colorings for your family,
sort of a reverse Converse. . . .''

Eugenia being piratical, and frank about it; there had been
a time when this would have amused him.

"She's not," deliberately, "a cousin at all. Adopted."

"Oh. Twice? Now by you?" She didn't quite like his silence
and became brisk. "I stopped by at the Flagship for a drink
and had a nice chat with Jule, mostly about you, she adores
you. And she's been telling me her memories about your Uncle
Phip, and family oddments, and seeing Sophie up here just last
Sunday. . . ."

The weeping—Sophie. Why?

"And darling, I would most dearly love to have a drink with
you. And maybe you can set me straight about Garrett, whether
it's a rumor or not."

He could see her, nostrils quivering, relentlessly following
a story, not solely because of its news value but because of its
Eugenia value. Her delicate brashness was both feared and
applauded in Washington.

"I'll be with you in half an hour. More or less."

Hand on the knob of his door, he paused. Under the overloud
radio from Vin and Glenna's room, he heard sounds so slight
they almost weren't there, a door opening, just the faintest
creak, the click of the latch on another door, the one across
the landing leading to the outside stairway. The careful lack
of noise implied secrecy.

He followed quietly. The remainder of the light was an
ominous dense gray-purple, low cloud overhead flying from
the northeast. Garrett had shed today's country-gentleman
tweeds and wore the dark suit he had arrived in. He was hatless,
the wind lifting his thick hair, but Jack saw in the hand holding
the attaché case his black homburg.

He was walking very fast to his rented Mercedes, parked
four cars or so down the road.

Jack fell in stride with him and he turned, started, and said,
"What the hell?" He had obviously had a great deal to drink

but was carrying it splendidly; he drew himself up in a tower of indignation that was burning its way into rage.

"Exactly," his nephew said, "That occurred to me, too."

"You interfering bastard, if you think you can stop me—" Before Jack knew what was coming, he was struck with powerful savagery and stumbled back in startled pain, just saving himself from falling.

"For Christ's sake, Garrett, what is this?"

Garrett was panting. "Sorry." He took out his handkerchief and wiped his face. "Too many things too fast—I had a call just now from Washington. A fire to put out. A meeting and then . . . I'll be back in time for the funeral. I have certain commitments, you know." He tried for a man-to-man smile. "Remember, your little trip from the Flagship when four would be a crowd. . . ."

He was being told, he supposed, that among his other activities Garrett was due in a Washington bed tonight, you know how it is, fella. He went down a mental list: Mrs. Jarman, the natural-gas heiress; Garrett's secretary, Leonie; or the ambassador's wife. Women still melted to the senator. He had divorced his second wife ten years ago and was free to dispose his attentions generously.

Well, some ruthless and intrusive phone calls could be made later, if Garrett was to be allowed to get away. But how could he be stopped in any case?

Perhaps in reaction to his own surge of violence, Garrett swayed a little.

"Are you all right driving your car?" Jack asked. "I'm heading into Provincetown myself in a few minutes. Or if you think I'm apt to drop you at the police station, can I get you a taxi?"

Can I get you a taxi, Garrett, to help get you to your meeting, and your bed, and/or to St. Stephen's Green in Dublin.

"I am quite all right driving my car, thank you, dear boy," Garrett said, enunciating every word with care. Jack stood watching him, unaware that he had his own palm pressed hard and cool against his throbbing jaw, while Garrett opened the door, got in, slammed it, and with great dexterity and flair backed up a few feet, made one quick turn, and went at a speed somewhere between modest and determined down the purpling windswept road.

Concluding her New York phone call, Kate said, "Yes, then, probably tomorrow night, but a short evening—good night, Ferdie."

"I wouldn't be so sure of that," Jack said immediately behind her. She felt the quick brush of a kiss on the nape of her neck. "And I wasn't eavesdropping. I just happened to be here."

His near and vibrant presence, in this house which had become a rather frightening place, somehow shadowed in spite of its warm bright lamplight and blaze of flowers, was of enormous comfort.

"Maybe, Ferdie," he said. "And maybe not. I have a day or so of leftover vacation still, and I'd planned to see you home to New York. No detours and no interruptions this time, Kate—all the way home."

She looked up into his eyes and found the depths in them too intense; and she didn't know how to read them.

Politely and inadequately, she said, "Well, that's very nice of you, Jack."

"He's a nice fellow any way you look at it," Father McAloon said cheerfully, at their elbows. "Are we all ready for the rosary? I'm a bit early but I have a meeting with the Catholic Daughters I wouldn't miss for the world," and he gave Jack his slow wink.

"But first, if you don't mind, Miss—Ms.?—Converse, I'll have a word with the man."

"Does that," Jack asked, leading him into the dining room, "mean a drink?"

"No, not until after prayers." But he gave the bottles and glasses a look of thirst. "I've been having qualms of conscience. You asked me, if you recall, whether I'd heard or knew about any . . . attachment of a sentimental nature between your uncle and Mrs. Grahn, and I said no. The thing is this, I thought it was nothing to be gone into with him there in his coffin, at peace. . . ."

Jack, feeling no compulsion to wait until after prayers, poured himself a drink and then, with a glance at the rosy face, poured another one.

"It'll loosen your tongue, Father," he said.

"I don't know how much there was in it. But naturally I hear things. I had an old aunt once, the only warm one in the family as far as money went, who changed her will when she was ninety and left everything to her doctor. Oh, it was a blow, I'll tell you. And she was a kind woman and sane as they come."

He took a large gulp of his scotch. "In any case, I thought it was my duty to let someone in the family know." There was no mention of the bequest to his church, and none was needed. "Leo was in Albany and I remembered I'd had a nice game of golf this summer with that big fellow—"

For some reason Jack didn't want to press for the name of that big fellow.

"Vincent. Vin."

"And when was it, weeks ago when you called him?"

"No, as a matter of fact it was last Saturday night."

Vin would have spread it around, the ghastly rumor, very fast, told everybody he could reach. Wouldn't he? Of course he would.

"And now," Father McAloon said, looking affectionately at his freshly emptied glass, "let us pray."

The Converses were a varied family in their degree of piety, their churchgoing habits, and their beliefs or disbeliefs. But they were, by early training and long habit, graceful and unself-conscious about observing the outward forms of their religion. Down on your knees, chant the responses to the Our Fathers and Hail Marys and Glory Bes in voices low and uninflected; there was nothing of hypocrisy in this, but a seemly pattern of good behavior. This was the way Phip wanted it; this was the way Phip would have it.

Sophie had repaired her makeup, but there was a recollection of tears in and around her eyes.

Tike had changed from her little-girl flowered dimity into a football jersey and tight white jeans. Timothy's cream suit, collecting grime and wrinkles, had so offended his father that he had borrowed a brown flannel suit of Phip's, too short at the ankles; he had surprised Leo by being unexpectedly docile about this.

Kate and Jack knelt together, right behind Marcia's tired rigidly upright back. Odd kind of intimacy, murmuring prayers side by side, but intimacy it was. Kate had no earthly idea which decade they were on, and on what Sorrowful Mystery they should be dwelling.

They were in a half circle near the coffin, their faces candle-lit and for the time composed and closed. Father McAloon's voice was rounded, soothing.

". . . As it was in the beginning, is now, and ever shall be, world without end, amen."

Only Vin and Glenna were missing. And Garrett.

TWENTY-FOUR

"Kate, I want a walk. I need some wind. Will you be my date for twenty minutes or so?"

He had appeared immediately after the rosary was concluded, trench-coated and erect and in some way rested. He looked ten years younger, blue and fair and black, his eyes curiously sparkling, merry, a Vin she used to know.

"Unless you have been previously booked for this time segment by John A. Converse."

"No, he's gone off to"—why was it difficult to say the name?—"Eugenia—Pell, isn't it?"

Afterward she had trouble remembering exactly what they said to each other on the cold windy moors. It was at once easy, familial, touching, and in retrospect unbearable.

There was something splendidly releasing about keeping up with his long fast stride, and having the air tear at you, defy you so that you had to bend against it and fight back while your blood raced to keep you warm and strong.

"Mind heading over to the sea? It ought to be something, with the northeast wind—I remember going over once in winter, I was getting over the flu and Phip asked us up, said the salt air would do me good. Those wild white horses, in January, roaring in—"

"I don't know, the sea . . . the wind will be . . ."

"You're not afraid to walk along a cliff with me, Kate?"

A gust almost took his words. "I'll hang on to you nice and tight."

It was hard to think, when you were being blown about this way. She had an idea that this was one of the most important split seconds of her life, but she didn't know why.

"No, Vin, of course I'm not afraid."

"I suppose you're thinking of that poor Spiggott."

"You can't help it. One moment browsing through asters and berries, and the next—"

"Well, that's life."

"No," Kate said, "that's death."

"Don't write copy at me, Kate dear."

Their heads were close together so they could hear each other comfortably. It was almost dark, ink-purple now, but there were no trees to bump into, no roads to cross.

"Where's Glenna, and how is she?"

"Peacefully pilled in our room, I hope, it's been one hell of a time for her and of course for everybody else."

There was a riotous crashing, very near and far below them, and the thunder and thump of some tremendous uneven muffled drum.

Vin got a flashlight out of his pocket and switched it on and then off.

"We're a good twelve feet away from the brink. . . . Do you suppose if we sat down with our backs to the wind we could manage a cigarette?"

"We could try."

Match cupped deep within his palms, he studied her cheek and her lowered lashes.

"This is beside the point, any point, young Kate, but I've always loved you, not just liked you, loved you."

"Vin—" This was no place, this drama of sound and unleashed windy violence, for a plunge into emotion.

"Even when you were a kid you were a nice fire crackling on the hearth, and then, you always did laugh, never failed me, when I thought I'd said something funny. I don't mean . . . love, so let's run away together and dump everything . . . I mean *love*, safety of some kind. Money in the bank. Christ, I can't seem to get away from the rustle of dollar bills, but do you know what I mean?''

"Yes, I think so." Impossible not to come to meet him. "You're very . . . dear to me, Vin.''

He put an arm around her shoulders and kissed her forehead.

"What was that?" Her spine stiffened.

Secretive as the purple air was, she knew that the moor dimpled down, just ahead and to the right of them, cover for somebody, anybody, lying flat, listening. But how silly, and why?

"Rabbits, probably, it's too late for snakes and they don't inhabit the moors anyway. Or maybe Spiggott's ghost—"

"Shouldn't we go back now?"

"You go back, Kate, take the flashlight, I want more air, and the sea sounds good, and I've had my fill of flowers and the fine art of embalming.''

He looked, or rather felt in the very vague outline of his features she could see or guess at, as if he wanted to be left alone. She was about to turn away when he said, "Just one thing to remember, Kate, *I'm* the note.''

She was bewildered and for the first time frightened.

"The note on the blackboard?" *Vin did it.*

"No. I'm my own note." He laughed and gave her a gentle shove in the direction of the house, perhaps half a mile away. "I'm reasonably sober, no matter what you may think about my ramblings. But see you have a drink waiting for me by your fire, J and B, double.''

She walked away very fast, hands in pockets and head bent, in flight from something she didn't at all understand. Certainly not from Vin.

I mean *love*, safety of some kind—

It could have been two minutes or five before she heard the hard distant ringing crack carried on the wind, and wildly thought at first she had been shot at, and stumbled and fell, and then knew what it was, and ran and ran, gasping, sobbing, someone's tearing voice in her ears, Oh Vin, oh Vin, oh *Vin*. . . .

Her foot went deep into a rabbit hole and she fell again, hard.

The jolt against earth and grass shook her out of hysteria.
She got to her feet and stood still.

Should she go back?

Maybe someone shot at *him*.

Maybe he was hurt, crying out for help, blood pouring—

Maybe someone else was out on the moors or in the far
pines—the night, after all, didn't belong only to the two of
them, to death, tragedy—someone after rabbits, or deer.

The hunting season had begun and the scrub pines were a
favorite haunt of the deer. But at this hour? People, though,
did cruel things with flashlights.

Maybe in that case he was fine, still striding, thankfully
gulping the salt air.

I need wind. The sea sounds good.

Stupid to panic, base and cowardly to run in the wrong
direction. Just because, for a blinding moment, when everything seemed to fall or crash into place, she thought Vin had
sent a final message on the wind.

I killed him and now it's my turn for me.

I'm the note. Suicides usually leave one. For note, read, my
remains.

A shadow to her left and a little behind her turned into a
person. Her arm was gripped and she felt an immense thankful-
ness.

Glenna.

The hand tightened savagely. "What was he saying to you?
What did he tell you?" No, not Glenna herself, but someone
who in ways resembled her. Someone sending out waves of
animal fear and—what?—menace.

"Glenna, he may be in trouble, we'd better—"

Glenna's voice knifed across hers. "What kind of trouble?
Why should Vin be in trouble?"

"I heard a shot—way back there—"

"Don't give me that. The woods are full of guns this time
of the year. Don't you dare try to get away from me," as Kate
made an attempt to wrench her arm free. She felt in the other
woman a rising, boiling rage and violence.

"Why in God's name should I try to get away from you?"

"Tell me what he said," Glenna cried. *"What did he tell you?"*

One of them had to simulate some kind of calm in this little core of madness.

"Not very much . . . that he wanted air . . . and how he'd been always fond of me, I suppose funerals, death, bring these things out . . . and something about a note. . . ."

"He gave you a note?"

"No—" and then another shrieked *no* as the blood sensed awful danger before the eye could find its shape, a swinging, something in the air above her head, a terrible thunderous pain at the back of her ear . . . falling, falling into the snow in Connecticut, Timothy's snowball with the frozen rock-hard apple in it, "Dirty, *lousy.* . . ."

"And what were you doing, Mr. Converse, intrepid reporter and responsible family member, when all hell broke loose in North Truro?"

A bitter question asked by himself to himself and as bitterly answered: "Oh, I was having a drink with a girl I know, at the Provincetown Inn, trying to find out if she was up to any television mischief and not just hanging around for a funeral because it was the proper thing to do."

"I have the funniest feeling you're not listening to me at all," Eugenia said, in their corner in the bar. "Are you mentally on the velvet kneeler taking a last look at your uncle? Or perhaps roaming fairer fields—what's that girl's name?"

Her voice was soft and summoning.

"I was just wondering when Jenkins was going to get in touch with you," Jack said thoughtfully into his glass, and then, "Speaking of calls, I must make one." He went to a telephone booth and dialed Phip's house.

To hell with extrasensory perception, the fire somewhere in his rib cage—too much to drink or too little sleep, probably. But call anyway, say hello to Kate, he hadn't talked to her over the phone for years and it would be interesting to hear the slightly different timbre of the transmitted voice—

Sophie answered. "Yes, everythin's fine here, for the livin', that is, but it would be nicer if you'd come back and decorate the premises. . . . Kate? She's gone out somewhere with Vin, I heard him say he'd like some fresh air and would she be his date unless you had the priority in that department."

"How long," he asked carefully, "have they been gone? Did they go in his car, do you know, or on foot?"

"Walkin', I think, at least they went out the back door and I figured they were off to the moors. Better them than me, in this wind. How long? Maybe twenty-five, thirty minutes, but my time sense is—"

There was some sound of commotion, and Sophie's drawl hurtled into a deafening scream in his ear, "Oh no, oh Jesus God, *Kate*—" and there was a crash that identified itself through a black haze: the receiver hitting the floor.

TWENTY-FIVE

With the heel of his palm on the horn, he drove at the top speed the Ford could summon, ninety-five miles an hour, slightly less on the curves, from Provincetown. He was in a peculiar kind of control of himself, one Jack directing the other Jack, the first in a suspended kind of despair and the second tough, seasoned with blood and disaster and ruin. All in a day's work.

He was halfway to North Truro before he remembered that he had left Eugenia at some table, without explanation and without farewell.

He was quite sure, not that it mattered, that she would be following him; that she would know where he had been snatched to.

But Kate— It's one thing to find yourself loving a woman, and on the edge of total commitment. But it would also be nice if you had a chance to get to know her.

The dark seasoned man said, The worst she can be is dead.

After that he stopped thinking and just drove. It did occur to him that his madman's speed on such a road might be one way of getting the police on his tail and on the scene, without stopping to make a telephone call.

Peter Jenkins still had his arm around Kate. Blood leaked from somewhere in her hair, down one side of her neck, staining the shoulder of her water-green jersey. She was conscious and able to stand upright, move, walk, but was staring as if she had arrived at some house of strangers and wondered what she was doing there.

"Doctor, Marcia," Sophie said to her aunt's stricken face. "*Call* him, Marcia, name of Littauer, I think, he'll be in the book. The *telephone* book, Marcia. . . . Here, Mr. —"

"Jenkins. Peter Jenkins. That woman —"

"Yes, in a minute, can you help her up the stairs? Good . . . just lie down, Kate honey, Leo, don't loom that way, can't you see she's terrified of everybody — do go, all of you, I've got your hand, Kate, everythin's goin' to be fine, somebody please get a towel from the bathroom —"

Leo, handing brandy in the dining room, said in a bewildered way to Peter Jenkins, "I always forget that with women it's first things first. What the hell *happened?*"

Jenkins found it hard to make a great deal of sense himself.

"That woman — she wasn't content with the blow, and there was a doorstop or something, shaped like a cat — iron — inside the pocketbook she whammed her with — the bitch was hard at work with a scarf, I think she was going to strangle her, but of course when she ran off I couldn't follow her because I thought this one — Kate — had had it, but after I'd picked her up and sort of carried her for a bit she came to, thank God, and . . ."

"Get your brandy down, man, and then we'll get on with whatever it is you have to tell us," Leo said. He glanced at the camera slung over Jenkins' shoulder. "I don't suppose you —"

"You bet your life I did," Jenkins said with fierce joy. "One when she swung that murderous bag and another when the strangling or whatever she was up to was beginning, I thought at first she was only trying to stop the blood. . . . I don't think she even knew I was there, and maybe she thought the flash was lightning, or the wrath of God coming down upon her, if I ever saw a woman beside herself, fresh out of a cage —"

"How is it," Leo asked, "to begin at the beginning, that you were at the scene of the attempted crime, if I may so put it?"

"I heard, I was told, something big might happen around

here, and I was just wandering, listening, trespassing if you will. . . .'' Warmed by his brandy, he grinned at Leo. ''Did you know that your brother the senator hit your nephew Jack? I lost that one, I didn't dare use a flash, not with those two—''

The front door exploded inward.

''Where is she—is—?''

An articulate man who suddenly could not speak, could not bring himself to ask the only question in the world.

From the doorway Marcia said, ''Someone is coming, I'm not certain who, all I could tell them was that she'd been struck by something . . . someone . . . and that there was a great deal of blood. . . .''

''What I want to know,'' Timothy said, ''is, who is *she?* Who is this who's fresh out of a cage? Where's Tike, by the way?''

''Upstairs,'' Leo said to Jack. Normally not disconnected in his utterances, he went on, ''Not Tike, that is, but Kate, Sophie's with her, this man brought her back to the house, she's been attacked but that is at the moment as far as we have progressed from a factual point of view. And she is very much alive last I saw.''

Jack seemed to manage the steep stairs in one leap.

Sophie said, ''Well, thank God, First Prize back on the scene, here's her hand, I think she's all right,'' and with delicacy, ''If you don't mind takin' over as nurse I'm dyin' of curiosity and will take myself downstairs, to see what Saint George of the Camera has to say for himself.''

There were two bloody towels under Kate's head. ''It's stopped, almost,'' Sophie reassured him, and closed the door behind her.

To the terrified shine of blue two inches from her own eyes, Kate said, ''Vin.''

''No, love, not Vin. . . .''

He didn't dare touch her, thinking she might break or explode or vanish in air, or die.

''Vin.''

''What is it, then?''

''Someone should go and look for him, I think he may be

hurt, or dying, or dead.'' Clear voice, low, too calm.

"Did he do this to you?"

"Vin? No." As he watched, the helpless tears of returning reaction, of coming with pain back from the white distances of shock into here and now, and who and what, poured out of the corners of her eyes and down her temples. "I think he . . .''

"Don't talk."

Marcia opened the door and said, "Littauer's at the hospital, he sent another man, a Truro man, he's here—Doctor, this is Miss Converse, who's been hit in the head, Jack, you'd better come downstairs and let the doctor take over. . . .''

Eugenia entered the house in a cautious glide, just as Jenkins was saying to Jack, "She's probably still out on the moors if she hasn't jumped in a car and gone off—''

"Jesus, who?" Jack said. *"Who?''*

"I don't know her name, somebody's wife, dark short hair, tan pants, and a hell of a big red and blue silk scarf which probably has blood on it—''

A dulled young voice from the doorway.

"Glenna, it sounds like," Timothy said.

"But where's Vin?" Jack asked, feeling his way around inside a nightmare that had no plot to it. "Kate said he might be dying, dead—''

Almost absent-mindedly, he went over to Eugenia and removed her shoulder bag. She often carried her tape recorder in it.

"Some way or another, it's all over, isn't it," she said, pale remote blue eyes on his.

"What's all over? She'll be—''

"Not Kate, I didn't mean that, I heard, I called here when you left me flat, I had a word with Peter—and of course I don't mean us, nobody has to write things out for me and get them notarized."

She went over to Peter and put an arm around his plaid waist. It wasn't going to be said, ever, that in a room with men in it Eugenia Pell had to do without.

"I mean, your Uncle Phip." She gestured toward the shadowy living room. "He's what it's all about, I somehow gather. And in one way or another it's over."

"Not entirely," Leo said in a voice urging action however unpleasant. "Jack?"

"Yes—but not until Dr. whoever it is comes down."

Dr. Whoever-It-Is said, "We'll want an X ray immediately, just to be sure, but I think she got off by an inch or so, I don't think there's serious damage, or concussion. However, just to be sure, and safe—"

On the word "safe" he looked surprised at himself. No one had told him why an attractive young woman had been struck savagely on her head. He knew about the funeral, and a little about the Converses. She had seemed to him perfectly sober, these people looked civilized, he couldn't imagine anything like a bottle fight in this charming house, over a man or something.

"Will she need an ambulance?" Marcia, efficient in her confusion, her exhaustion.

"No, a car will do nicely."

"I'll drive her to Hyannis," Sophie said. "And, darlin's—if you're goin' out there to look, take care."

It wasn't care that was after all needed; it was stomach.

Vin dead high over the sea, half his head shot away.

Glenna sprawled over his body, weeping in a final pain and woe, her blood all over him. She had, it emerged later, taken the gun from his hand and used it inaccurately. In her case, an ambulance was needed. It wasn't until the early hours of the morning, in Hyannis, that she died.

In their awful journey over the moors, she said the awful things, not in sentences but in gasps.

Vin had arranged everything so nicely for her and she had to go and spoil it.

He'd killed himself because, in their bedroom, after she blew up in the kitchen, after she saw that it was he who was to be hunted down, and branded, she couldn't stand it any more, and told him that she hadn't spent the night with her mother, she had driven up to North Truro and—

Her words: "smothered Phip. With two huge pillows. I think the Irish word is 'burked.' How he fought. Vin wanted to know, when he saw me stark, about the bruises, and I said I'd been taking karate lessons at the club. But it was all for him. For *Vin*. And the killing thing is that everybody thought he'd done it and I couldn't even give him a safe clearance. . . .''

He had left her, he thought, asleep, she said. "He went out looking like some kind of goddamned gorgeous saint, but marvelous, the way he was years ago. . . .''

She got up and watched from the window as he and Kate, close against the wind, climbed the slope under the aspens.

"Vin can't keep things to himself . . . after all, he's in the word business . . . I thought he had to get it out of his head, tell her about it, and then I thought there would be no end to it. . . .''

Jack, in harsh pain himself but physically intact, said against his will, "Spiggott?"

The anecdotal voice was much lower now, failing.

Spiggott hadn't been, really, a problem. Vin was out with Garrett, and she had worried about him, Spiggott, after putting her ear to the office door on her way to the bathroom.

"I needed cigarettes and I thought I'd walk down to the crossroads. And I saw that woman waiting for him in his car, that Grahn woman. And, it's really funny when you think of it, I saw him spot her and turn away as if the devil was after him, and come to think of it he was . . . I was . . . and then, to get back to Kate, she having a conference with the sister if Tike was right, and then she and Vin having another conference out here. . . .

"But, Spiggott. I figured that if anyone saw or heard us on the edge of the cliff I'd say he attacked me, maybe wanted to rape me even at my advanced age, and I just *pushed*—it would be lucky if he died and if he didn't I'd have my threatened-virtue story all ready . . . but you know, it was very fortunate, he did die,'' this in an airy voice that had lost any connection with life, or listeners, or self.

Later Jack thought that it was very fortunate for Glenna that she, too, did die.

Leo had gone to answer the telephone when there was a brisk knock at the door that sounded familiar.

Police Chief Dutra said politely, "I hate to bother you again at a time like this, but the way they're yakking in town, and just for the book, I'm going to have to ask a couple of questions."

There was a sound something like laughter, but not mirth, from Jack. He said, "Yes, well, you timed this right, Chief Dutra. . . ."

Kate found, in the car, that when she started talking it was hard to stop.

Sophie drove evenly, carefully, and her winces were invisible but strongly recorded by her passenger.

"I'm sorry, Sophie, I'll try to shut up now."

"Well, you've had the floor till, what?—Brewster. To take your mind off your troubles I'm goin' to talk a little. Trivia. It'll be good for both of us."

They were in Vin's Cadillac. "More comfortable for you," she had insisted when Kate had balked. "And God-blessed Vin wouldn't mind."

She pressed the lighter on the dashboard, lit her cigarette, and said, "Will you believe it that for a few crazy hours I thought my no-good father was alive and well and murderin' in North Truro? I suppose he'd still be in the will if extant, that's what that house, that's what our upstandin' family did to me. And look what it did to you. You thought—maybe for only twenty seconds or so, sittin' in that green silk chair in my room—that I was Mrs. Murderer."

"No, Sophie, I didn't, but—"

"But you thought I was not tellin' the truth, the whole truth, and nothin' but the truth. You were right. Cataclysms starin' us in the face, I'll complete my own short story. I was up here Sunday with a man. *The* man. The money statement was bible, but I left him out because he's in the process of divorcin' a wife who wouldn't look kindly on the company he keeps. . . . It was a crazy thing to do but I hadn't seen him for three weeks, he had to be in London, and you know how it is, or do you?"

"Yes," Kate said. "I know exactly how it is."

Her X ray was negative.

"I figured that," Sophie said. "Nobody without all their

buttons could have made everythin' that happened out there so ghastly clear. You'd better call the First Prize right now and take him off the hook.''

While he waited for them, he went reluctantly and grimly into Phip's office, took the cover off the Olivetti electric portable, thumbed the switch on the left, typed, Please omit byline, and then under that, NORTH TRURO, MASS., Oct. 15. The body of Vincent Converse . . .

TWENTY-SIX

On doctor's orders, Kate did not attend her uncle's funeral. But she got a concise professional report.

"Jammed, standing room only. Of course, it's a small church. Mobs outside, and some faces I recognized, don't be surprised to see your relatives in *Time* and *Newsweek* as well as the papers. And, well, you saw it from your window, sheets of rain and a horrible northeast wind. Thank God Phip spared us the solemn requiem, McAloon raced through the mass, but everything perfectly proper, he looked in a state of shock.

"Garrett didn't make it and in a way I don't blame him. His resignation hit the deck, in case you haven't seen the papers, handing over the Banking Reform Committee to his vice-chairman, ill health and so on. I don't think they'll go the expense of an investigation now, particularly as their bird will have flown. What I didn't tell you before was that he paid an enormous sum by Sealand Banks to leave them alone. . . .

"I think Phip would have been amused by one of the altar boys, he had on firemen's red socks and flowered sneakers. Leo was in the pew behind me. I heard him mutter to Timothy, just before mass started, 'That picture is valued at approximately three hundred and fifty thousand dollars, we will, needless to say, subtract it from your pittance.' And naturally I followed that one up, a much bigger haul than Tike's apostle spoons."

"Tell me," Kate said, looking for some of Sophie's relieving

air-clearing trivia, "about Timothy. I don't understand him at
all."

"I have a theory about Timothy."

"Oh?" Eager for shrewd enlightenment about her bland,
contained Indian-looking cousin, she waited.

Leaning close, as one who is about to impart a piece of rare
and priceless information, Jack spaced each word carefully.

"I have a theory," he breathed into her ear, "that Timothy
is an enigma."

And was pleased at the laughter that caught her; he had been
worried and was still concerned about how she was going to
come out of this.

They had just fastened their seat belts on the plane for New
York, at Logan Airport. First class was sold out, occupied by
a mysterious group of Koreans.

"But don't you have to stay and, and cover it?" she had
asked.

"No, they're sending up someone else, under the circumstances. A more objective point a view."

He bundled his raincoat and hers on the rack. "You sit by
the window, Kate, I don't mind the middle one, or not very
much, and maybe by the grace of God nobody will sit on the
aisle."

He handed her his batch of newspapers while he attempted
without a great deal of success to accommodate his long legs.
The batch flopped open, and on top was a tabloid with a large
photograph of Tike in her white satin painter's overalls kissing
Phip in his coffin.

Model Niece Mourns Murdered Millionaire.

"Yes, I saw that at the newsstand," he said to her stunned
face. "Tike's friend. He sent the negatives to the papers just
in case. If you read on, you'll find 'photographs taken in the
early hours of a morning that was to develop into a day of
triple tragedy, by famous fashion photographer Robbin Roy.' "

"Sophie said she was trashy."

"She is, first, last, and always."

He looked up in horror as a very tall and very fat woman
plumped herself overflowingly down in the aisle seat beside

him, just before takeoff. She opened a voluminous tapestry
bag and took out some hideous knitting, marbled pink and blue
and yellow wool, and got immediately to work.

"Would you mind," Kate whispered, "holding my hand
during takeoff? It always makes me nervous. . . ."

Marvelous hand, dry, warm, bony, strong. It was the most
untroubled roar down the runway of her life. The plane seemed
to lift almost instantly, not take half an hour or so about it.

The woman stared at their linked hands.

Then, from a distance of about a foot, she began a minute
scrutiny of his turned-away dark head, his jawline, his collar,
his tie, his free and shapely hand, his shirt cuff showing a
gray-and-white-striped inch, his square gold cuff link. The fact
that there was an elderly-girlish admiration in the eyes did not
make it easier.

Jack turned his head and, pressing a button for the stewardess
and having to rise and loom over her to do this, gave her back
a blue and blinding stare that seemed to have no effect on her
whatever.

"Four martinis," Jack said to the stewardess. "Two large
glasses, with ice. An olive, Kate? Yes, olives."

Kate took her own closeup of the face turned to her. Pale.
What fair skins the Converses had. He looked older. There
were shadows in his eyes and under them. The creases flanking
his mouth; that she had attributed to a certain merriment, looked
deep, thoughtful, and sad.

She knew without being told that the hands and the fine
mouth wanted her.

For now, anyway.

Click, went the intrusive needles. Click. What terrible garment was being produced? It looked like a sweater for a very
large baby.

In a fast funny rage that she thought she might be going to
have to—delightfully—get used to, he turned to the knitting
woman, first looking pointedly over his shoulder at the many
empty seats behind them.

"Madam, may I trouble you to change your seat? My client
and I have legal affairs to discuss, if you don't mind. And

there are seats going begging." Feeling her busy elbow poking
his arm: "You could really . . . spread out."

"I like it here," the woman said stolidly. "This is the seat
they gave me, anyway."

"They won't, you know, open an emergency door and dump
you out if you do change."

"This," she said, programmed, "is the one they gave me.
You have no right to turn me out of the seat they gave me."

"Well, knit away, do, although there must be a certain savor
missing. As far as I know, no one is going to be beheaded."
He reached out his hand to Kate. "If this lady will not, we
will. Excuse us."

Holding in healing laughter, hiding indecent joy after awful-
ness, after death—she couldn't help catching the feeling from
him—Kate accepted his hand and observed that he trod deliberately upon the edge of a huge foot in a luggage-colored
open-toed sandal.

The large woman howled with pain. "Oh, sorry," Jack said.
"Close quarters, wasn't it? If you wouldn't mind handing us
our drinks?"

"What legal matters?" Kate asked, as they settled in their
new, private seats toward the rear of the plane.

"Well, a license, blood tests, all that kind of thing. I don't
mind living in sin with you until we're passed through the
machinery but we might as well make it formal as soon as
possible."

"Formal . . ." She was in what she told him later was an
O'Donough fever. Quite different from the Converse calm.
"But not, you don't mean—I really never intended veils and
tuberoses and things—"

He gave her an amused and loving glance.

"Neither did I. No, I mean we've been getting married to
each other ever since, when?—Thursday morning. It's all taken
care of, except for"—he took her hand and put his lips to the
back of it—"various interesting completions. And you'll just
have to brace yourself. It's a rather spectacular mess of a family
you're marrying into, Kate."